MW00488305

Don't Shoot the Messenger

Ashara D.

For my Darling Trinity,

Mommy, Daddy, Aikea and Adriana: I love you all.

Acknowledgments

First and foremost, I would like to thank the Lord above for blessing me with the gift of writing, and even at times when I wanted to give it up, not allowing me to quit on my true passion. I want to thank my parents, Jeffery and Connie Mills, for without their love, I would not be here, sharing pieces of me with you. Thank you, Donald Walters, for the cover design of the book and your thoughtful feedback. I want to give a special thank you to Tiandria Wright and Pennie Womack. You ladies just don't know how your persistent reading and feedback kept me going and gave me inspiration to keep writing. I also owe many thanks to my sister, Aikea Mills, my best friend Dede Olive, Andrea Holloway, Ashley Jones, Tamika Ellis, and T Hampton. All of you have in some form or fashion given me encouragement to not give up on my dream. There are so many people, family and friends, I could thank because God has placed an abundance of great people in my life, so if I didn't name you specifically, just know that I do thank you. In the words of my late, great Uncle Mike, "Later, later." Enjoy!

Chapter One

"Paula, we've been together for a very long time and I've never loved anyone as much as I love you. With that being said, I think it's time we take a break."

5'10" Sean Campbell stood in the large handicap stall in the men's restroom at Charlie's Restaurant staring at his confused reflection as he attempted to memorize his speech. He was at dinner with his long-time girlfriend, Paula Davis. They had been together since their sophomore year of high school and were now supposed to be celebrating their ten year anniversary. A whole decade of love and happiness. Well, they were happy for most of those ten years, but what young couple doesn't go through periods of drama and brief separation? Hell, what older couple for that matter? But the important thing was that through it all they had survived, and that day was their day to celebrate, right? Wrong.

If you asked Paula, her and Sean's relationship was stronger than it had ever been. But for Sean, that night was no celebration. There was no doubt that he loved Paula with all of his heart and there really was no one else that he had ever loved more than her. But that was just it; she was the *only* woman he ever loved! At the tender age of twenty-five, he'd been with Paula for almost half his life, and all of his adulthood. Sean was yearning for a dip in someone else's pool, a taste of someone else's cake, a twist in someone else's ignition. He had been with Paula since high school for goodness sakes! Sean wasn't exactly all holy and old ye faithful one all ten years, though. The couple broke up on more than one occasion, and Sean had even had sex with another girl, Monica, during one of those separations. At the time, though, Monica was a virgin and sex with her was like parking a Hummer H1 into a compact vehicle space; he had to ease into it. She squirmed a lot and that was no fun for him. When the lovers entered college, they made a verbal commitment to remain faithful to one another. Sean didn't have sexual intercourse with another woman, but there were some nice oral exchanges and make-out sessions on more than one occasion. However, he made it very clear that he was not leaving Paula to be with anyone else. Now, Sean wanted more; he was ready for a change, but he just couldn't seem to let go of all the precious memories. He remembered exactly how he and Paula got together as if it had happened yesterday.

It was Thursday, October 13, 2005, two days before the homecoming dance and Sean didn't have a date yet. There weren't many girls that he was interested in at his school, and if they were cute enough, they already had a boyfriend. He had asked

Jasmine, a girl who he thought had a thing for him, but Marcus, who was a little taller and whose popularity status was a little higher, had already beat Sean to the punch. He thought about just going by himself. He was good looking and was sure that if he went alone, he wouldn't leave alone. His Hershey's chocolate skin, dark brown eyes and average build didn't quite knock the ladies off their feet. But his smile, that's what did it. The embarrassing braces he wore throughout his middle school years had paid off. His smile was so bright, it made his eyes shine even in the midst of darkness. And that's what mesmerized the ladies.

Paula was new to the city of Orlando and had transferred to Riversdale High School from Ranier High School in Oklahoma City. She was an army brat back then, so her family had moved a few times before. She had only been a student at her new school for a few months, and the couple of guys who had already asked her to the dance she turned down with the quickness. But Sean didn't care. He was confident in his approach. He stepped right to Paula during lunch, after the English II class they shared. She was sitting at the long, yellow, rectangle shaped table with a group of her new girlfriends. Sean walked right up to the table, looking like an imitation Morris Chestnut. He sat in an empty blue chair and politely interrupted the conversation the girls were having.

"So, Paula, are you going to the dance Saturday?" he inquired looking directly at her.

"Yeah, I'm going. Who wants to know?" she asked. Truth was, she did find Sean attractive and was hoping he would ask her to the homecoming dance. That's actually what she and her friends had been talking about before he'd rudely interrupted them. Paula's friends all had dates already and they didn't want Paula to be by herself.

"I wanna know. Why else would I be asking? So, will you do me the honor of being my date?" he boldly asked her in front of everyone. The cafeteria walls seemed to close in and it got really quiet as if everybody awaited her response to the proposal.

Michelle kicked Paula's foot underneath the table and Angie gave her the, "Girl, you better say, 'Yes,'" look. Needless to say, Paula agreed to attend the dance with him and they had been almost inseparable ever since. And now, there Sean stood, in a bathroom stall ten years later, ready to give it all up.

Looking back on it now, it seemed that he had gotten a little soft over the years, pillow soft. But the soft spot was for Paula and always had been. He was her pillow every night, literally. It wasn't that he didn't love her anymore; he just needed a dose of reality. The relationship seemed to almost shelter him from the real experiences of life. He just couldn't imagine going through life having had sex with only one girl. Well, one and a half. What kind of loser does that? At the same time though, he didn't want it to seem like sex with other girls was his only motivation for wanting to leave. He just wanted to experience life without Paula to see if being with her was where he really wanted to be.

After they graduated high school, they made a promise to each other to be committed and to never cheat, and if they were unhappy in the relationship to just be honest with each other. He was having the urge now more than ever to experiment with other women. Sean had been as faithful as he thought any man could be transitioning from a teenager into adulthood.

Now, staring in the water-spotted mirror, Sean could barely stand the sight of his own face. He felt like a coward, a punk, a little bitch, all because he didn't have the balls to be a man and just break up with Paula. But, it is what it is. He had to be honest with her and tell her it was over. He twisted the right knob on the sink for cold water, cuffed his hands together to fill them, and doused his face in it. He grabbed two brown paper towels, dried the specs of water off his face and exited the restroom, making his way back to the comfortable dimly lit corner booth where his beautiful girlfriend awaited. It was about to go down.

While he was gone, Paula had ordered a pair of strawberry lemonades for them, but upon his return, she could tell something was bothering him. She was thinking maybe she should've ordered alcoholic beverages instead. Sean had been acting strange and quite stand-offish for the past couple of weeks, but every time she tried to talk to him about it, he always assured her that everything was okay. Paula figured that he might just be stressed out from work. He was one of the managers at a local Publix grocery store. He had earned his degree in Business Management, but Publix wasn't exactly his idea of the perfect career. Plus, the new general manager was an asshole. But a job was a job and money was money. It paid the bills.

"You okay, babe?" Paula asked, knowing in the back of her mind that he would just say, "Yes."

He surprised her when he said, "Well, actually there's something that I want to talk to you about." He was trying to keep his speech memorized in his head without looking like he had too much on his mind.

"What's up? You know you can tell me anything," Paula said, reaching out her manicured hands as a gesture for Sean to meet her halfway. Paula always kept up her appearance. She worked as an interior designer, and people don't trust you with the design of their house if you're not well put together yourself.

He grabbed her hand and cleared his throat. "Paula, we've been together for a very long time and I've never loved anyone as much as I love you."

His palms began to sweat. He gently pulled his hand away from Paula's and rubbed his hands together under the table to eliminate the moisture. He could feel the perspiration begin to leak from his underarms. Not to mention the pounding of his heart and the rate at which it was beating. He had lock jaw; his mouth was filled with little white cotton balls. A cat literally had his tongue. A black cat. Damn. *I'm having a heart attack*, he thought.

Paula, being the optimist that she was, thought he was trying to propose or something and maybe he was getting cold feet at the last minute. Patricia, Paula's mother, had been bugging her about when she and Sean were going to tie the knot. Now Paula had the wedding bug, but she didn't want to pressure Sean. She knew they were still young and had plenty of time. Trying to break the ice, she smiled at him, and surprisingly he was able to crack a nervous smile back.

"I love you, too," she told him.

Since he had gotten so quiet, she decided to disclose the anniversary gift she had gotten for him to lighten up the mood.

"Well, I know we're supposed to wait until after dinner to share gifts, but I have to tell you now before I bust! So, you know Angie started working at Carnival a little while ago and I finally got her to hook a sista up. Drum roll, please!" She began to beat the palms of her hands on the table to create the desired sound effect. "We're going to the Bahamas! It's still costing me a pretty penny, so this is an anniversary and Christmas gift." She was so excited to finally spill her guts about the trip and her demeanor was contagious. Sean's speech was dead meat.

"Wow! Damn babe, that's what's up!" Now Sean felt like an even bigger bitch than before. But how could he pass up a trip like that? They had never been on a cruise before.

When the waitress returned, they ordered their food and Sean tried to enjoy the rest of the evening, and did indeed. He pushed his feelings back down deep within the pits of his soul and decided to put the break-up on hold. While Paula ate her chicken Alfredo, Sean ate his steak and loaded mashed potatoes and they laughed the night away. On a night that was supposed to be no celebration, it turned out to be one of the biggest celebrations the young couple had shared in their ten years together. But Sean knew the next time he spoke to his best friend, Damien, he was definitely going to get clowned.

Chapter Two

The almond colored skin that covered his 6'2" frame and athletic build was damn near edible. One look and you were hooked. If his body could speak, it would say, "Eat your heart out." No one could deny that Damien Johnson was a fine piece of meat, and he used his looks for any advantage he could get, especially with the women.

A mixture of ebony and ivory, Damien had his parents to thank for his curly brown hair and hazel eyes that he used to subdue women to his bedroom. He was a pure ladies' man. They all loved him and he didn't mind letting them sample a piece, even two at a time sometimes. Damien made it very clear that he did not want to be in a committed relationship. Lust and leave – that was his motto.

He couldn't understand for the life of him how Sean had managed to be handcuffed to one woman for so long. To Damien, that was like being in jail. He liked Paula; she was a nice girl and all, but damn, they'd been together since they were sophomores in high school. It was time for Damien to hook his boy up with some new booty.

Sean and Damien had always been opposites though, ever since they met in the sixth grade. It was August of 2001 and the first day of school had just ended. A crowd of adolescents in the Boys and Girls Club gathered outside on the basketball courts.

"Hey, look at the nerd with his shirt tucked in. Look like he 'bout to go sell my daddy some insurance!"

All of a sudden, there was a burst of laughter from the crowd of kids.

"Yo' broke ass daddy can't afford my insurance," Sean replied to the big bully Brian.

The crowd's reaction went from laughter to a deep "Ooooohhh" sound that seemed to echo off the bleachers and cause a riot of black birds to abandon their post on a tall light pole to fly in formation across the sky. Brian's face turned red with fury as he physically confronted Sean. Just as his fat fingers began to bend into a fist, hot stuff Damien strutted up with his red Jordan basketball shorts, red, black and white Jordan 12s, and Spaulding ball under his arm.

"Man, leave him alone," Damien told Brian.

"Who you supposed to be, his body guard?"

"Forget him. I'm here to kick your butt on this court." Damien tossed the ball into Brian's gut then let it drop and bounce back into his hands.

If there was anything that Brian liked better than being a big bully, it was basketball, even though his skills on the court were piss-poor.

Damien handled his business on the court and Sean watched every grueling minute of it. That was the day their bromance began. They wanted nothing but the best for each other and always had each other's back whether the water was calm or the tide was rough. As it stood now, the water was calm and Damien felt it was the perfect time for Sean to let go of his life saver and take his surfboard for a test drive.

Damien knew yesterday was Sean and Paula's anniversary, but he hadn't heard from Sean in two days. He also knew Sean was trying to break it off with Paula, but he had a funny feeling that Sean didn't go through with it, or else he would've called by now. Damien picked up his phone to call his best friend to see what was going on. Locating Sean's name in the recent call log, Damien slid his finger to the right and put the receiver to his ear. The phone rang twice before he heard a voice on the other end.

"Hello?" Sean could already sense what was coming.

"What's up wit' cha?"

"Nothin' much man. Just over here chillin'," Sean answered.

Damien could hear Paula in the background asking Sean where the remote was.

"So you punked out, huh?" Damien cut straight to the chase. He always kept it one hundred with his friends and this time was no different. He was tired of Sean always complaining about wanting to hook up with other chicks, yet he wouldn't break up with Paula. And although he had technically stepped out in the past, he wasn't interested in cheating on Paula. He did have a conscience and a few values and morals.

"Man, I ain't no punk. I just need a little bit more time, that's all," he tried to reason with Damien.

"I know what that means. That means she got you something good for your anniversary. Nigga, I know how to read between the lines," Damien replied, laughing.

"The anniversary gift ain't got nothing to do with nothing! But we are going to the Bahamas next month."

"On a cruise?" Damien inquired.

"Yeah."

"I knew it!" Damien yelled in the receiver. "You a lil' bitch! You don't wanna break up with that girl. You couldn't handle it out here in the real world

17

anyway. Being a ladies' man ain't easy. Like they say, 'It's hard out here for a pimp,' and you don't have the heart for it," Damien told Sean, trying not to laugh too hard, but at the same time not trying at all. Next thing he knew, he heard a *beep* and the line went dead.

Sean was so pissed that he had hung up. He couldn't really be mad at Damien, though; he was just telling the truth. After Paula had told Sean the good news about the mini vacation to the Bahamas at dinner, he couldn't turn around and break up with her. Then she would have to try to cancel the trip, which may even be non-refundable, and he wouldn't dare put her through that. What kind of man would he be if he made her waste her money like that? So, the only logical thing to do was to hold off on the break-up and just enjoy the trip, right?

Damien didn't know why Sean was so upset with him. Deep down, Damien could really care less whether Sean and Paula broke up or stayed together. He was just tired of hearing about it. Plus, he had his own personal issues to deal with.

Damien's phone began to vibrate and music shot from the speakers. He figured it must be Sean calling back, but when he saw the image on the screen, it was one of his younger twin brothers, Donovan.

"What's up, bro?" That was his way of saying, "Hello?"

"Hey, man. You busy? I need a ride to work," Donovan asked desperately.

"What do you mean you need a ride? You have a car with four wheels, an engine, and a steering wheel just like me," Damien replied sounding aggravated.

"It won't start smart ass. And Mom's the only one here, but she's locked away in her room and I don't wanna disturb her. I think something is bothering her. So, can you please just take me? I'll figure out what's wrong with my car when I get off," Donovan replied, trying to sound as calm as possible.

"You cutting into my gym time, punk. I'll be there in twenty minutes and you better have some gas money," Damien said right before hanging up the phone. Not only was Damien a ladies' man, he was also extremely cheap, but frugal was the word he preferred to use. He was always looking for a payment whenever he lent his personal services to others. He had a lot to learn about being humble.

After dropping Donovan off at the barbershop where he cut hair, Damien decided to skip the gym altogether and go back to his parents' house to check on his mom, Deborah. She hadn't been acting like herself as of late and Damien wanted to get to the bottom of what was bothering her. It was almost as if she was falling into a state of mild depression. If there was anyone whom Damien loved more than himself, it was his mother and he wanted nothing more than for her to be happy.

Pulling up into the driveway and parking his navy blue Mazda in front of the three-car garage, Damien got out and fumbled through his key ring to find the key to the front door of the three thousand square foot ranch style home. Following a sleek and curvy walk-way, Damien made his way up the front steps and unlocked the door to the home he and his younger twin brothers grew up and shared so many memories in.

Damien locked the front door behind him and made his way to the right, past the dining room, the kitchen, and the laundry room, then down the short hall to his parents' bedroom. Damien turned his head and placed his left ear to the door softly, but heard nothing. He slowly turned the knob and slightly pushed the door forward. Well, Donovan hadn't been completely right; Mom wasn't literally locked away in her room. But there she lay, in the middle of the king-sized bed, surrounded by a heap of pillows.

"Mom?" Damien spoke softly.

"Damien!" she popped her head up and turned around to see her eldest son. After the initial shock faded, she smiled, happy to have some company. "Hey son. What a nice surprise," Deborah started smiling.

"Yeah, I figured I'd stop by and check on you. Everything okay? I brought something for you," Damien said as he held his hands behind his back, keeping the surprise concealed.

"What's that?" Deborah asked enthusiastically.

Damien's hands came out from hiding and into view came two vanilla milk shakes in a cup holder from Chick-fil-A. His mom loved those shakes and she always requested two cherries on top of her whip cream. Her face filled with laughter as he handed her the cup and a straw.

"You always know how to put a smile on my face." Her eyes glowed as she looked up at her son.

The two sipped on their shakes in silence for a couple minutes until Deborah finally unleashed the elephant in the room.

"Your dad is having an affair," Deborah looked at her son square in the eyes as she delivered the startling news. There was no need for her to beat around the bush. Damien was not a child and was grown enough to handle such information. But handling and believing were two different things.

"What? Are you sure, Mom? I don't think Dad would—"

"He is," Deborah said sternly, cutting Damien off mid-sentence. "I have not physically caught him in the act, but I know. It's a woman's intuition. As cliché as that sounds, it's true. I can feel it; I just know it. And he changed the password on his phone."

By now, she had gotten up out of bed and was ambling around the room. Damien's eyes went from following his mother to looking down at the floor. He noticed a dark stain on the tan carpet and began to wonder how long it had been there. Then his thoughts shifted to how long he and his family had lived in that house, and how long his parents had been together. There was no way in hell his father was being unfaithful, at least not in his mind. He needed proof, hard-core evidence that something was going on. Until then, he would console and comfort his mother when needed, but he secretly disagreed with her.

"So what are you gonna do?" You can't leave him, Mom." Damien sounded almost as if he was pleading with her.

"I can and I will if I feel the need to. You boys aren't babies any more. You're young men and plenty old enough to know how relationships work. I don't know what will happen, but you should be prepared for anything." Finishing her last word, Deborah sipped some more of her milk shake.

Damien was at a loss for words. "Alright, Mom. Well, I gotta go run some errands, so I'll check on you later." He kissed his mom on her right cheek with his cold lips and then left. Following the same path, he made his way back to the front door, locked it on his way out, and walked to his car. He sat in the driver's seat for a minute thinking before finally cranking it up. His dad couldn't be cheating. Tim loved Deborah, and Damien had bore witness to that all his life. He finally came to the conclusion that his mom was trippin'. He turned the key in the ignition and drove off.

Chapter Three

Paula could see Angela and Michelle talking, laughing, and taking sips of water as she made her way to the corner booth where they awaited. Paula bumped Angela over with her hip and butted in.

"Sounds like y'all are having too much fun without me."

"Oh, look who finally decided to show up, Miss Bahama Mama herself," Michelle joked.

"Whatever. I'm not that late," Paula replied, rolling her eyes then sneaking a glance at the gold watch on her left wrist.

"So, spill it. How was the trip?" Angie asked inquisitively.

"Forget that! Where's the ring?!" Michelle demanded.

"Dang, blood hounds! Can we get a drink first?" Paula suggested, not quite ready to share that there was no ring and she had no idea when one would be coming. The problem with being the only chick in the clique with a man for Paula was that her girlfriends were constantly hounding her about when she and Sean were going to take the next step in their relationship, especially now that it's been ten years.

Paula loved Michelle and Angie, almost like sisters, particularly because she grew up with no siblings. But sometimes, sisters are annoying and they just need to mind their own damn business. This instance was a perfect example.

"Okay Michelle, let's get her drunk first. Then she'll tell us everything," Angie laughed.

When the waitress returned, the three ladies ordered their first round of Apple Martinis. It was sure to be an interesting night. Too much liquid sensation always made Paula open up and become transparent to the human eye. She wasn't much of a drinker for that very reason, but she felt comfortable with certain people, and her girlfriends fell under that category of people.

Once the drinks began to flow, so did the conversation about the events of the cruise. Paula shared with Angie and Michelle the exciting vacation that she and Sean had just returned from. According to Paula, they had the time of their lives. They swam in the pool, put on their singing voices for karaoke, got their laugh on at a comedy show, tested their old school Motown knowledge in a music trivia game, went cruise clubbing, and even went to the spa and got massages together. And all of that was just the ship activity. Best of all, though, was the intimacy. Paula and Sean's relationship hadn't lacked sex, but it lacked passionate sex. Something about being in the middle of the ocean brought back the passion that had been missing.

After the third round, Paula began to open up about Sean's recent behavior. She expressed that she could sense that something was up with Sean, and she was positive she had it all figured out. Sean wanted to propose; he was just nervous. Angie and Michelle just took their drunk friend's word for it, but they both gave each other "the eye" like they knew there was more to the story.

The topic of conversation changed several times throughout the night while the girls ran back and forth to and from the restroom sobering up before parting ways. They gave each other invisible cheek kisses and promised to text each other once they made it home safely.

As Paula drove home, she listened to the smooth grooves of Star 94.5. Marvin Gaye's "Let's Get It On" faded away and after a brief moment of silence, Donnell Jones' "Where I Wanna Be" began to play. Paula sang along out loud in her car, not realizing that those lyrics were the very words that Sean wanted to say to her. Pretty soon, that song would become her reality. Not knowing what lay ahead, she sang, word for word.

Chapter Four

Sean made his way through the aisles making sure the shelves were stocked neatly and properly. Then he walked up to the registers to assist with bagging. During the week, especially on a Monday afternoon, there weren't too many employees on the schedule, so managers had to help out.

Melissa's line was the longest, so that's where Sean went. He stood at the end of line four bagging groceries for a few minutes before he felt a tap on his left shoulder. He turned to his left, but saw no one there.

"Boo!" Damien popped up on the right side of Sean.

"Man, I'm trying to work," Sean said laughing. "What are you doing here?"

"What normal people come to Publix to do, grocery shop," Damien replied sarcastically.

"Now you and I both know you're a Wal-Mart man. Publix run too deep for those pockets of yours."

"Damn. Why you gotta call me out like that? Maybe in addition to grocery shopping for things that are buy one-get one free, I came to check on your big head ass. You haven't told a brotha nothing about your lil' cruise," Damien replied.

"Thank you for shopping at Publix. Have a great day," Sean spoke to a customer as he placed the last bag in her buggy. Then he turned to Melissa and said, "I'll be back in a few."

Sean gave Damien a shove and the two began walking towards aisle two, the bread aisle.

"The cruise was straight, man. We honestly had a good time. I just feel like I'm sending her mixed signals and I don't know what to do," Sean explained to Damien.

"Man I'm tired of you acting like a big ass baby. Either you do it or hell, I'll do it for you," Damien demanded with a slight laugh.

He didn't get a response right away. He looked at Sean and noticed that something, or someone, had caught his eye. Damien turned around to see what Sean was staring at, and it didn't take him long to figure it out.

She was slim and tall, about 5'9". Even in sweat pants, a hoodie, and boots, she was phenomenal. Her brown eyes glowed in the light and her short haircut elongated her smooth neck, making her look like a model. She and Sean locked eyes for a few seconds before Damien cut in.

"Yeah, you like what you see, don't you? But naw, what about Paula? I love Paula. I can't hurt Paula. Blah, blah, blah," Damien mocked Sean.

"Man, just 'cause I'm not a womanizer and heartbreaker like you doesn't mean I'm a lil' punk," Sean quietly yelled at Damien.

"Don't make this about me. Now like I said, either you can do it or I'ma do it, but we're gonna stop talkin' about this shit and start being about it."

"Fine!" Sean shouted back. He looked to see if the girl was still standing there, but she was gone. He stormed back to Melissa's line to help bag.

Paula loved her career as an interior designer. She had been working for three years and her clientele had greatly expanded during that period of time. She advertised herself well, had an amazing website that displayed her best work, but the best thing of all was the word-of-mouth. Her clients were very loyal and always spoke great things about her to others.

That was how she acquired her new clients, Mr. and Mrs. Williams. Mrs. Williams had called her before the cruise and Paula promised to visit the Williams' home as soon as she returned. Mrs. Williams had heard about Paula from a good friend at church, so she decided to give her a try. She and her husband had just refinanced their home and they wanted to do some renovations to the kitchen and both the master and guest bathrooms.

Mrs. Williams and Paula had spoken on the phone about some of the details, so Paula already had some designs and colors in mind. She just needed to see the space and layout to iron out the rest.

Paula pulled up to the entrance of the gated community where the Williams lived. Mrs. Williams had previously given her the four-digit number code, so Paula entered them and patiently waited for the gate to slide open. She slowly drove over the bright, yellow speed bump then turned right as the GPS directed her to do. After passing three beautiful homes, she spotted the older woman standing outside whipping her hands through the air. It was Mrs. Williams. Paula maneuvered her car alongside the curve, parallel parked, and got out with materials in hand.

"You must be Paula," Mrs. Williams greeted her.

"And you must be Mrs. Williams," Paula replied.

"Please, call me Mrs. Patty." The ladies embraced and Mrs. Patty led the way into her home.

She gave Paula a tour of the four bedroom, three bathroom craftsman style home. As they made their way around the house, Mrs. Patty pointed out the three main areas that she wanted Paula to focus on: the kitchen, guest bathroom, and master bathroom.

Paula noted that the kitchen was a surprisingly great space to work with. It just needed some updating: new cabinetry, appliances, countertops, and flooring. With Paula's touch, Mrs. Patty would have the gourmet kitchen she'd always dreamed of. She reached down in her bag until her fingers felt the grooves and curves of the yellow measuring tape. She needed accurate dimensions for each area she would be putting in plans for renovating.

The same was true for the master bathroom. With improved lighting, a double vanity, updated shower and separate tub, and new flooring, it would be much more serene and spa-like.

Paula and Mrs. Patty sat at the round eat-in kitchen table and discussed all the details about the upcoming renovations.

"Is there anything that Mr. Williams wants in particular?" Paula asked Mrs. Patty. He was at work and was not able to voice his own opinion, but Paula was hoping Mrs. Patty wouldn't mind speaking on his behalf.

"Well, he wants a massive shower with multiple shower heads that release the water like a rainfall. He saw it on HGTV and said he had to have one," Mrs. Patty smiled.

"With your $30,000 budget, I think I can handle that. You'll both love the finished product," Paula replied.

The two then discussed details about the layout, patterns and color schemes of the kitchen and bathrooms. Mrs. Patty wanted the best for the kitchen: granite counter tops, a new island added in the center of the kitchen, new cabinetry, stainless steel appliances, a unique backsplash, a deep farmer sink, and tile flooring. For the master bathroom, she wanted new countertops, his and her vanities, recessed lighting, a new tiled shower, and jet tub to soak and relax in.

"I'll be in contact with my contractor and they should be able to begin working within the next couple of weeks. I'll give you a call with the exact day we'll begin and we'll also get all the paperwork squared away," Paula explained to Mrs. Patty. "You all don't plan on staying here during the renovations, do you?"

"No. All that dust will stir up Darryl's allergies. We're going to stay with our daughter and her husband, but we'll be by periodically to check on the progress," Mrs. Patty responded.

"Okay. Sounds like a plan."

The women stood up and slowly began to walk to the front door. Mrs. Patty seemed to glow with excitement now that the plans were finally in place. She escorted Paula to her black 2005 four-door Honda Civic. The ladies waved good-bye and the meeting was adjourned.

Paula quickly grabbed a bite to eat for lunch before going to check on the renovations for another client.

The water began to boil rapidly and the steam began to rise. Paula poured the rotini noodles into the pot and sprinkled a dab of salt on top. She stirred them with a black plastic spoon and let them boil for a few minutes before stirring again. She was preparing a delicious pasta meal for dinner. Paula liked to cook at least two to three times a week. Between leftovers and eating other quickly prepared light meals, she and Sean didn't have to spend too much money on fast food.

Just as Paula was about to put the hamburger on to cook, she was startled by the ding-dong of the doorbell. She wasn't expecting any company and Sean was still at work. She strolled to the door all while wondering who it could be. Standing on her tippy toes, she pushed herself up so her eyes could see clearly out of the peephole. It was Damien. Paula rolled her eyes before opening the door.

"Hey. Sean's not home yet," Paula said directly with the door only slightly ajar. It may have come off as kind of rude, which was unintentional. She didn't dislike Damien. She just thought he was a low down, dirty dog.

"Yeah, I know. I actually stopped by to talk to you. May I come in for a minute?" Damien asked as nicely as possible. He knew that Paula probably didn't want to let him in, so he was trying to be polite.

Their relationship had always been rocky. Paula, of course, knew about the bunches of women Damien kept up his sleeve. She also knew about the time he tried to persuade Sean to cheat on her, and ever since then, she'd kept her distance from Damien.

33

"Oh. I guess. Come on in." Paula stepped to the side, allowing the door to open up more widely, and let Damien walk in. She looked a little baffled, but went back to the kitchen to continue cooking. "You'll have to excuse me. I'm in the middle of preparing dinner."

"It's cool. I don't wanna interrupt. I really don't even wanna drag this out so I'm just gonna jump straight to the point," Damien looked at Paula's back as he spoke. She was turned away, facing the stove, so he couldn't see the sour look on her face as the each word came out of his mouth. But his last sentence made Paula stop and turn around. She wondered what he needed to get straight to the point about.

"Umm, what's up?" The room was getting hot and Paula was starting to sweat, but it wasn't because of the heat from the kitchen.

"Have you noticed that Sean has been acting a little strange lately?" Damien asked Paula inquisitively.

Paula's shoulders relaxed a little. She felt reassured that she wasn't imagining the fact that Sean hadn't been acting like himself as of late.

"Yeah, I have noticed. And he's been a little short with me, too. Do you know what's going on?" Paula questioned Damien in a serious tone.

"Well, yeah I do, actually." Damien dropped his head and took a deep breath. "I know you and

Sean just celebrated your ten year anniversary, and that's all good. He loves you, he really does, but—"

"Is he cheating on me?! Did you pass one of your little hoes over to him and it actually worked this time?!" Paula harshly interrupted. The spatula she had begun to cook the hamburger with was suddenly slammed into the counter and the noodles were beginning to overcook.

"No, Paula. He's not cheating on you. But—"

"But what?!" she cut in again.

"But he needs a break!" Damien began to slowly approach Paula, but he saw the drawer where the knives were located and the hot boiling water on the stove, so his feet stopped moving, but his mouth didn't. "He loves you and he's been trying to break up with you, but he just doesn't want to hurt your feelings. I mean damn Paula, you thought it was gonna last forever? It's been ten years! He's a guy!"

"So let me get this shit straight. Sean wants to break up with me? Why? So he can be a male whore like you? This was probably all your idea, wasn't it?" Paula accused Damien.

"No, it wasn't. This is all on him. He just wasn't man enough to tell you, so here I am, taking matters into my own hands." Damien pounded his chest with his right fist and threw his hands in the air.

Paula could see the train speeding down the tracks. She could hear the loud *choo choo*s and she could feel the steam about to exit through her ears.

"Bitch, kiss my ass! Get outta my damn house!" Paula came out from the behind the kitchen counter, spatula still in hand, and began to push Damien towards the door.

"Don't get that damn hamburger grease on me!" Damien tried to dodge the spatula as Paula swung.

"I said get out!" Paula screamed at the top of her lungs. She began pounding the spatula in the middle of Damien's back as he approached the door. A grease stain was starting to form on the back of his shirt.

All of a sudden, Sean burst through the front door. He could hear all of the commotion as he neared the house.

Paula's eyes began to rage with fire at the sight of Sean and she turned her spatula beating and yelling toward him.

"Oh, so you wanna break up with me?!"

"Paula, hold on! Wait a minute!" Sean tried to plea with her while trying to block her swings.

"No, I will not wait a minute. You tell me and you tell me now. Is what he said true? Do you want to break up with me?"

Sean's eyes shifted from Paula to Damien and finally to the floor. There was a brief moment of silence before the words came slithering out of his mouth.

"Yes. Yes, it's true. But I can explain," Sean tried to reason with her, but it was of no avail.

"Just leave. Both of you just get the hell out," Paula pointed to the door as she spoke.

The two men left without saying another word, and Paula locked the door right behind them. She back pedaled to the couch and plopped down on the center cushion. Her head migrated to the comfort of her palms as she sat there in disbelief at the scene that had just played out.

Her silent thoughts came to an abrupt halt by the sound of the smoke detector going off. Dinner was ruined. More importantly, the life that she had grown so accustomed to and her relationship with Sean was now ruined as well.

Chapter Five

Every first Sunday of each month, the Johnson family gathered to break bread together. Ever since Damien moved out to his own apartment and the twins were young maturing men who were going to be legal soon, Deborah wanted a way to ensure that her tight-knit family wouldn't go their separate ways. The best guarantee of that was food.

The way to a Johnson man's heart was definitely through his stomach. Well, at least that had proven to be true for the three Johnson boys. For Tim, however, Deborah was sure that the way to his heart was a new piece of ass. That had seemed to be true for the past few months and Deborah was ready to put it to an end to it.

It had almost become a nightly routine for the couple to debate over Tim's alleged infidelities; Deborah with her accusations and Tim with his constant denials. And no make-up sex afterwards. It was serious. The Dead End sign at the end of the road was becoming more visible each day.

Dinner consisted of baked barbeque chicken, fried chicken, baked macaroni and cheese, string beans, and buttery flavored Hawaiian rolls. It would be guzzled down with a pitcher of homemade lemonade with fresh slices of lemons. Finally for dessert would be a frozen Sara Lee apple pie that Deborah was ready to pop into the bottom half of the double oven.

"Don!!!" Deborah screamed loud enough for the neighbors to hear.

She could hear Donovan's feet as he approached the kitchen.

"Yes?" Donovan answered.

"Is Damien on the way? The food is ready."

"Yes. He texted me about ten minutes ago and said he was on his way," Donovan informed his mother.

"Okay. What about David? What time does he get off?"

The sound of a car engine pulling up in the driveway redirected their attention. Deborah cut a center hole in the apple pie and placed aluminum around the crust's edges before gently placing it on the center rack in the oven. Donovan went to go see who had just arrived.

"You sure you don't wanna come? Some good soul food might make you feel better," Damien tried to sell Sunday dinner, but Sean wasn't buying.

"I'm good. I think I'll go by the house and get some clothes."

"You sure you don't need no back-up? It could get ugly," Damien replied.

"Can't get no uglier than the other night. This is long overdue, anyway," Sean reassured Damien.

Like magnets, their fists connected, and as they demagnetized Damien headed for the door and Sean reached for his phone. He didn't have to scroll down long before Paula's name and image appeared in the log. He called without hesitation, but as the phone began to ring, his pulse began to increase. After five rings, the voicemail came on and Sean ended the call without leaving a message. He tried to be optimistic and figured it was a good sign that she hadn't sent him straight to voicemail. He grabbed his keys, deciding that he would go gather some of his belongings now, whether Paula was home or not.

Damien arrived just as the twins were setting the table and Deborah was preparing everyone's plate. He slapped David over the head as he pranced with haste to the kitchen to greet his mother.

"Hey, Mom."

"Well look who finally decided to show up. You know I don't like to wait around," Deborah said sternly.

"I know."

"Wash up and take these plates to your brothers. Then come back and get yours," she directed him.

Damien stood over the kitchen sink and pushed the faucet up to turn the water on. As the water flowed from the pipes into the sink and down the drain, Damien lathered his hands with vanilla scented soap, giving the water a minute to warm up. He rinsed his hands, causing little bubbles to form in the sink. He grabbed a paper towel off the roll and dried his hands. Then he grabbed the two plates off the counter of the center island and took them to his brothers as he was instructed to do. He would normally nibble on a plate while delivering it to its rightful owner, but both hands were full this time. However, the aroma that traveled up to his nostrils from the food still had his mouth watery for a bite to eat. He would fight over his mom's food. Literally.

Once, when Damien was in high school and David and Donovan were still in middle school, there was a food fight about who would get the last piece of fried chicken. Tim had already had his second helping and there was only one piece of golden-brown heaven left and three growing boys who devoured everything in sight.

Donovan wasn't a fighter and tended to stray away from unnecessary confrontation, so he was the first brother to bow out of the chicken fight. And then there were two. Damien, of course, was the eldest and always used his age to get his way. This time, David wasn't trying to hear none of that age mess. He didn't care when their momma popped Damien out, he just wanted to satisfy his healthy appetite with another piece of deliciousness.

Damien was enraged that David hadn't backed down as easily as Donovan had. Damien was the oldest, damn it, end of argument. But David wasn't seeing the situation from the same vantage point. David wanted his older brother to realize that age wasn't always the deciding factor. The dual that they were about to partake in wasn't even really about the chicken, but more about the principles of brotherhood.

Needless to say, Damien defeated David that night. Turned out that being older, larger, and possessing more physical strength had the final say-so in the matter. So Damien took pleasure in eating that last piece of chicken, and as he did, he licked the grease from his fingers and lips in pure bliss as his younger brothers sulked in their misery of defeat.

Damien delivered the plates to his brothers and made his way back to the kitchen. Just as he was about to ask where his dad was, Tim appeared from around the corner.

"Hey Dad."

"Hey son." They embraced with a firm grip of their right hands leaning into a one-armed hug.

"Here, Damien. Grab your plate so we can go eat." Deborah grabbed her plate and led the way to the dining room table where David and Donovan awaited. Tim followed last in line, under the assumption that his plate was already on the table. He was quite surprised that it wasn't, and even though his face said it all, he didn't dare open his mouth to question Deb about it. He just made a U-turn and headed back towards the kitchen.

All three boys turned and looked at their mother simultaneously.

"What?" Deb questioned as she shrugged her shoulders. "Who's going to pray over the food?"

"I will," David answered. "Bow your heads and close your eyes."

Just then, Tim entered the dining room once more. A sense of frustration began to fill his body.

"Can I sit down first? Are you guys going to start without me?"

"Hurry up then," Deb snarled.

"Sorry Dad. You're just in time for prayer," Don reassured Tim.

Once everyone had their heads bowed and eyes closed, David began to bless the food.

"Thank you, Jesus. Hallelujah! Amen."

"Amen," the rest of the family said in unison.

"Pretty soon, the only sound in the dining room came from the forks scraping the bottom of plates and food being chomped and grinded in between teeth. During a chewing break, Deb decided to break the speaking silence.

"So, which one of my boys is going to be the first one to fill that empty chair with a female guest?"

The family sat at a rectangle shaped cherry oak table. Surrounded by six chairs, there was always at least one empty chair. Deborah and Tim sat at the ends directly across from one another, the twins sat side-by-side and Damien sat across from David. The chair adjacent to Damien and Tim was vacant. The boys all looked at the empty chair as if someone was really sitting there. Then they all looked at each other, smiled, and continued to stuff food down their mouths.

"Damien, you haven't found the apple of your eye yet?" Deb inquired.

"No, Mom. I'm not ready for all that yet."

"Well good because if you're not ready don't lead anyone on. And don't go cheating on them when you *think* you've found the next best thing." Deborah's eyes shifted from Damien to Tim.

Tim didn't look up to see her eyes on him before he began talking. "Oh, Deb, leave the boys alone. When they're ready, they'll know. And so will we."

"I'm just engaging in conversation with my sons," Deborah responded to Tim.

"Yeah, I know, but maybe we could change the subject."

"Well maybe you could choke on a bone."

"Deb, don't be childish."

"What's childish is you sneaking around like a little boy and cheating on me with some little bitch and acting like I'm supposed to be okay with it."

"Honey, can we please talk about this in private?" Tim pleaded with her.

"Oh, Timothy, don't honey me. Talking in private is what people do when they don't want their conversation to be heard by others. But I want our sons to know. I want the whole damn world to know that it's over. Me and you are done. Stick a fork in it!"

Deborah slammed her silver fork down into a piece of chicken, leaving it standing straight up. Then she shoved her chair back, stood up and stormed out of the dining room. The Johnson men were left sitting there, staring at each other, wondering what the hell just happened.

Since he had already somewhat had this conversation with his mom, Damien decided to be straight up with his dad and ask for the truth.

"Well?" Damien glared at his dad.

"Well, what?" Tim was almost flabbergasted.

"Did you cheat on Mom? *Are* you cheating on mom?" Damien questioned his dad in a serious tone.

Tim dropped his head, then inhaled and exhaled. "No and no. I love your mother. You boys know I love her and I wouldn't do anything like this to hurt her or our family."

Just then, the aroma of apple pie could be smelled in the air. It was almost ready. Tim used the opportunity to escape from the awkward stares he was receiving from his sons to go check on the pie. The doomed dinner was done and the dessert probably would be, too.

Chapter Six

Damien inserted the silver key into the hole of the front door. He could hear voices from the TV before he turned the key to the left to unlock it. The scent of fast food made his nostrils flare as he entered and shut the door behind him.

Sean awoke from his makeshift bed on the couch at the sound of Damien's keys hitting the glass coffee table. He quickly grabbed the Burger King bag off the table and threw it away. He was thankful that Damien was giving him a place to lay his head and he wanted to respect his best friend's apartment.

"Back so soon?" Sean asked Damien.

"I could be asking you the same thing," Damien replied.

"Paula wasn't home, so I just got some clothes and left," Sean said disappointingly.

"Why do you sound like a lost little puppy? This is what you wanted, right?"

"I mean yeah, but…I don't know. I just wish I didn't have to see her hurt like that. If you could've told her and I didn't have to see her, I think this would be easier. But anyway, why are you back so soon?" Sean went back to his original question.

Damien didn't answer right away. He pondered and his mind lingered on Sean's last words.

His eyes didn't blink. He was almost like a statue until Sean snapped him back to reality.

"My bad, man. Must've been daydreaming. But dinner was terrible."

"Terrible? Your mom ain't never cooked a bad meal. What are you talking about?"

"I mean the vibes at dinner between my parents. Moms thinks Dad is cheating on her," Damien shook his head in disbelief at his own words.

"Mr. Tim? A cheater?" Sean was shocked.

"Yeah man, that's what moms is thinking. But I don't know. My dad denies it and I want to believe him. He says he hasn't done anything wrong and my dad never lied to me and my brothers before."

"True. Well I hope they work that out," Sean tried to sound reassuring.

"Yeah me too, man. But I'ma head to bed."

"Aight," Sean replied.

Damien made his way to his bedroom. All he wanted to do was ease his mind and rest his body for the remainder of the night. He kept replaying the dinner scene in his mind. Then, all of a sudden, the memory of Paula smacking him with a greasy spatula came running across his head. He didn't even realize he had fallen asleep until about three hours later when he suddenly woke up. He sat straight up in the middle of his bed feeling like Garrett Morgan with a new invention to help save lives.

The time on his phone read 2:12am and he knew Sean had to be up early for work. It took everything in him not to go in the living room and wake Sean up, but he resisted the urge and eventually drifted back into a deep sleep.

It was another dull Monday on the job. Although it was where shopping was a pleasure for customers, it couldn't be any less exciting for Sean. He did his usual morning manager duties, then crept around the store, aisle by aisle checking for perfection of minute details. Were the shelves fully stocked? Was the food stocked in order of expiration dates? Were all cans and boxes facing forward so the labels could be seen? Check, check, and check. The last resort was for Sean to go assist with bagging, and that's exactly what he was down to – the last resort.

Sean strolled through the aisles once more and then slowly walked up to the register and check-out section. But before he could get settled at any checkout line, he glanced up to see Damien forcefully walking his way with a serious look on his face, yet a shimmer of light in his eyes. *This better be good*, Sean thought.

Damien grabbed Sean's shoulders, forcing him to turn around. "Walk and talk," Damien said. "Walk and talk."

"What the hell is wrong with you?"

"I've been thinking about this all night and when I tell you what it is, I don't want you to say nothing. I just want you to think about it and let me know what you think when you get back to the crib." Damien stopped speaking and stuck his right hand out and waited for Sean to extend his as acknowledgement of the agreement.

"Last night, you said something about wishing you didn't have to see Paula hurt. So, what if you didn't have to? What if you hired me to do your dirty work? What if you didn't have to see or do anything? What if we created a business for bustas, I mean people, in similar situations such as yours? What if people paid us to break up with their significant others for them?"

Damien stopped speaking once more and allowed his words to marinate. They stood in the bread aisle, which had somehow become the place for serious discussions. The silence only lasted for a few seconds.

"I have to run, so think about it," Damien said to Sean, who still seemed to be digesting the proposition that was presented to him. Just as quickly as Damien had walked in the store, he walked out with the same speed, the automatic sliding exit doors closing right behind him.

Sean used Damien's spare key to unlock the apartment door. Damien sat with his legs stretched along the recliner part of his two-piece sectional enjoying a PB&J and watching reruns of Martin on MTV2. They made eye contact before Sean closed the door and sat down on the other end of the couch. Jerome was about to be in the house when Sean broke in.

"I'm in."

Damien looked at him in disbelief, but that soon transformed into excitement. "Dawg, you for real? You really think it could work?"

Sean nodded his head up and down, then added, "I gotta give it to you, the idea may be a little farfetched, but it's great. There must be other people out there going through a similar situation. Of course, we'll have to iron out all the logistics and create a business plan, but yeah, I'm down to do business."

Sean saw this as a great entrepreneurial opportunity. He was tired of just being a manager at Publix, and he was really tired of working for "The Man" and under all the confines of traditional work. Successful people take risks in life and Sean was ready to do just that. He had turned over a new leaf. There was no Paula to try and stop him or reason with him. As a matter of fact, if this business venture worked out in the long run, he would actually have Paula to thank.

Damien, on the other hand, wasn't thinking about the process they would have to go through to start this business. Nor was he thinking about any long term effects it would have. The only thing on his mind was making money.

"First, we need a name," Damien said.

Sean went along with it. "Umm, The Break-Up Masters."

"A good name." Damien added, rolling his eyes.

"Leave Me Alone." Sean tried again.

"Something catchy that really describes what the business is all about."

"Dump Your Mate."

The two of them went back and forth, exchanging names on and off for a couple of hours in between eating junk food and watching TV. There were a few contenders that Damien had offered, but none that really appealed to them both. Sean's creative juices didn't flow so freely, but the last name that he threw out was the winner, hands down.

"Don't Shoot the Messenger."

And thus, their business was conceived.

Chapter Seven

Paula tied the thin white laces of the red and blue bowling shoes she had just rented into a knot. She pulled her long, black wavy hair back into a low ponytail that sat right above her neck before going to search for the perfect bowling ball.

Everything glowed neon bright colors in the dark. She searched and inspected bowling balls until she found the perfect size and weight. A pink one she tried was just the right weight, but her fingers would need lubricant to slide in and out. A green one with yellow abstract lines was far from a match. It was much too heavy and the holes looked like they were large enough to fit Shaq's hands. When she spotted a purple one, which was her favorite color, she knew it'd be just right, and it was. As she returned to lane five, Michelle and Angie came strolling through the sliding double-door entrance of the bowling alley.

Ever since the breakup with Sean about a week ago, Paula hadn't really reached out to anyone, not even her best friends. So when Angie called and invited her out for bowling, she figured it was time to stop sulking and accepted the invitation. Plus, cosmic bowling was one of her favorite pastimes.

When Angie and Michelle got their shoe rentals, they met Paula at lane five.

"About time you heifers decided to show up," Paula said as her eyes rolled from the roof of her eye sockets to the ticking clock on her wrist. They were the ones who invited her to go bowling and then show up late.

"Umm, you can't talk 'cause you always late *and* you been ghost for the past week. Other than these little one and two words responses to my texts, I haven't heard from your ass. So what is that about?" Angie demanded.

"Mmm hmm," Michelle added her two cents.

All four eyes were on Paula and she felt like she was being backed into the gutter, but she wasn't going for it. Not yet. Out of the three of them, she was the only one who was ever able to maintain a long-lasting relationship. In a way, she was embarrassed about the way things ended with Sean.

"I've just been really busy with work. I met with a new client this week, and I'm still finishing up with the Williams."

Michelle and Angie looked at each other, and Paula could see the doubt in their eyes.

"Mmm hmm," Michelle added two more cents.

"Whatever! Y'all ready to get beat or what?" Paula tried to change the subject, and momentarily, it worked.

Paula entered their names to display on the screen above while Angela and Michelle went on a short search for their bowling balls. They didn't have to go far before they returned to their lane. It was game time.

Paula was up first. She grabbed her size seven purple ball with her right thumb, middle and ring fingers, and placed her left hand underneath to secure it. She took her stance and eyed the twelve pins. One step, two, three, release. Gutter ball. The twelve pins laughed and taunted her on the screen as she walked back to retrieve her ball.

"That was just practice!" Michelle cheered Paula on for her next attempt.

The pins used to be her and Sean. Nothing could knock them down. Paula's purple ball spit out the machine and she grabbed it once more. She zeroed in down the middle of the lane. Her ball didn't curve like the professionals'. It followed an invisible straight line, sometimes straight down the middle, but most times veering to one side or the other. Paula took three steps again and watched the ball roll down the slippery surface. The middle pin, the ring leader, was in the bowling ball's path and wouldn't escape this time. Crash! Strike. Well, in this case, it was a spare. The demolition of the pins resonated and echoed in Paula's heart: A true representation of a love that once was. The lyrics to Selena's part in Kanye's song rang in her ears. It had all fallen down.

For the past week, Paula had done everything in her power not to think about Sean. She hadn't cried, but secretly, on the inside, she mourned every day. Tonight was different. Angie and Michelle cheered for Paula's spare, but as she turned around, her eyes glistened and glowed in the dark. The applause came to a halt and instead became outstretched and embracing arms.

"What's wrong?" Paula's two friends asked in unison.

Paula tried to contain the anguish she was feeling so that she could speak. Finally she said, "It's over. We broke up."

"What?" Angela questioned.

"Are you serious?" Michelle instantly followed up.

"It's over between me and Sean," Paula responded to them both.

"What happened?" Michelle continued to question Paula.

"He broke up with me." Paula added.

"He broke up with you?!" Michelle and Angie both yelled at the same time, sounding like Tia and Tamera.

"Yeah. Well, actually he had Damien do it for him 'cause he 'didn't want to hurt me.'" She held up quotation mark symbols with her fingers.

"Oh hell no!" Angie hollered, causing the people in lane four to look in their direction.

The girls quickly realized that the bowling scene was not the place to be. They agreed to make a quick pit stop at the local wine and spirits store before heading to Paula's place for girls' talk.

Sean and Damien arrived at Tim's place of business to seek his advice as a financial advisor. Over the past fourteen years, Damien's father had assisted hundreds of people chase their small business dreams, prepare for retirement, or simply just survive financially after a divorce.

Even though Tim was Damien's father, the two young men had to be sure they had their ducks in a row before asking for Tim's assistance. Sean and Damien wanted to show Tim that they were serious about this business venture.

The business plan was typed up and laid out in a professional-looking portfolio. All of the details, including the name of the business, the owners, the marketing strategy, the plan and execution for the break-ups, and the cost of services, were included inside of the portfolio.

Sean and Damien were also including a survey that they had conducted. They randomly surveyed one hundred people about their willingness to seek the services of Don't Shoot the Messenger, whether at the present time or in a relationship from the past. Twenty-six percent said they would definitely seek the services. Twenty-two percent stated that it was very likely. Ten percent were neutral about the matter. Twenty-seven percent said that it was not very likely and the last fifteen percent would definitely not. The results were just about split in half, but there was one important factor that Damien and Sean had noted. Most of the surveyors under the age of thirty were more likely to seek their services while surveyors over the age of thirty were not as interested. With this information, the two partners were able to select their target market.

"I see you gentlemen have been doing some homework. I like what I'm seeing," Tim smiled at Sean and Damien, and they smiled back.

"But," Tim added, "to be honest with you boys, this would be an extremely risky business to invest in. My calculations for profit are not predicting high amounts."

The boys' smiles slowly began to fade as Tim continued to speak.

"However, since I believe in your dreams and want to support the two of you, I will approve a small investment loan in the amount of five thousand dollars." This was the first time in his career that Tim was drastically mixing business and personal matters. There was just no way he could shoot down his son's dreams. Even if the business failed, it wouldn't be because he didn't invest.

Sean and Damien were relieved. They each had their own savings accounts, but they knew they'd probably run through those funds rather quickly.

"Thank you, Mr. Johnson," Sean stood up and outstretched his right hand to give Tim a firm handshake.

Before sitting back down, he caught a quick glimpse of Paula's business cards sitting atop of Mr. Johnson's desk. When Paula began working full time as an interior designer, the Johnsons invited Sean and her over for Sunday dinner. That night, she and Mr. Johnson exchanged business cards and have been referring clients to each other ever since.

"Thank you, Mr. Johnson," Damien repeated.

"Call me Dad," Tim said in response. All three men laughed in unison.

Just then, Tim's office phone rang. Just as quickly as he answered it, he attached the phone back to its receiver.

"Alright fellas, I've got another new client meeting and he's here early. I like him already," Tim smiled as he headed to the door. Sean and Damien followed his lead. He escorted them to the waiting area.

"Christine, can you please escort the boys to Keith's office to get the loan paperwork started?"

"Yes, Mr. Johnson, and this is Mr. Joseph Hall, your next appointment," Christine responded.

"You can call me Joe."

The two men firmly shook hands upon meeting, and Tim briefly introduced Damien and Sean before the two parties went their separate ways in the financial offices.

Back in Tim's office, Joe took a seat in the black leather chair that Damien had just been sitting in. The cushion was still warm from his body heat. The meeting began with some small talk between the two.

Joe shared with Tim that he was newly divorced and had only recently moved to the area. The parents of one daughter, the couple parted ways due to irreconcilable differences. Joe was under the impression that the female judge who handled their divorce case had some kind of vendetta against men, which was why his alimony and child support added up to what he thought was a ridiculous sum of money. So, now there he was, in Tim's office, seeking some professional financial management.

"Well, to help serve your needs a little better, I'll need to see the files Christine asked you to provide," Tim said as his eyes shifted to the manila folder in Joe's left hand.

"Right," Joe replied.

Opening the manila folder, he pulled out his first paycheck stub from the job he recently acquired, the last thirty days of bank transactions, the court order for alimony and child support, the lease to the condo he just purchased, and his monthly bills.

Tim took a few moments to glance at all of the paperwork.

"I see you work at The Law Offices of Moore and Brown. My wife's an attorney there."

"Oh, yeah? What's her name?"

"Deborah Johnson," Tim said as he turned around the picture on his desk for Joe to see.

"Oh, I have met her. Very nice lady. You're a lucky man," Joe said smiling.

"Thank you," Tim replied grinning. "Well give me a couple of days to sort through the numbers and I'll have your budget all set for you."

"Thanks, Tim."

Tim and Joe both stood up to shake hands once more. Before turning around to leave, Joe spotted a stack of business cards on Tim's desk for a home interior designer. Since moving into his new condo after the demise of his marriage, the forty year old was having a difficult time with how to furnish and decorate it. He was feeling like a bachelor in his twenties again, but he didn't want his home to look like it. Hopefully this interior decorator could lend him some assistance.

Chapter Eight

Sean completed the last details of the business Facebook page he created for Don't Shoot the Messenger. Pretty soon, it'd be published for the entire World Wide Web to see.

He and Damien had already gotten professional flyers and business cards made. The flyers could be seen throughout the entire city and business cards had been given to everyone they knew and any stranger on the street who would accept one.

They had also purchased an old, used white cargo van. If they needed to help someone move any large items, they'd be ready. Once they started to pull in some revenue, they would get the company name and logo painted on the van.

"Alright bruh, come check out this page before I publish it," Sean called out to Damien from the living room.

Damien appeared from his bedroom a couple minutes later in basketball shorts and a white tank top and plopped down on the corner cushion of his dark brown couch. Sean slid the silver HP laptop across the coffee table far enough for Damien to stretch and reach for it.

He glanced at the page momentarily, finally saying, "This shit is legit! If this goes the way we want, it's gonna change our lives."

Sean nodded his head in agreement. Damien returned the laptop to Sean; the only thing left to do was make the business page public. They both updated their own personal Facebook statuses announcing to all their friends to like their business page. Don't Shoot the Messenger was finally Facebook official.

"You ready?" Damien asked Sean.

Damien's mom had invited them over for Sunday dinner. Sean secretly hoped there would be another dinner fiasco like the one Damien told him about before. He could use a good laugh. Life hadn't been the same without Paula, even though it had only been a couple months. As much as he was ready for a break from her, he was beginning to miss her. He hadn't even been on a date yet. But there was one regular Publix guest that he'd had his eyes on. He'd seen her twice now and he was thinking about making that move the next time.

"Yeah, I'm coming," Sean replied. Damien locked the door behind them as they exited apartment 223.

The sun had met its peak and was now headed west. There was still a slight crisp among the early March air, but nothing more than a light jacket or long sleeve shirt was needed to guard the arms from the kisses of the wind. Florida weather was bipolar, but you could almost bet it'd be warm outside.

Damien sped the entire way to his parents' house. Sean despised riding in the same vehicle with Damien behind the wheel because he had a lead foot. The only time he ever eased off the gas was when he saw red and blue, which was surprisingly rare. To be the speedster he was, Damien had only gotten three speeding tickets in the nine years he'd had his driver's license. Sean, on the other hand, was a little more conservative. He got his first ticket at sixteen, not even one month after attaining his driver's license. His parents acted a straight monkey and his driving privileges were suspended for one month. Not to mention he had to find a job to work and pay his parents back for paying the citation, plus interest. He realized then that speeding wasn't worth all that shit. He hadn't gotten any more speeding tickets since then, but still found it baffling that Damien only had three.

Sean grabbed ahold of the handle above his head on the passenger side as Damien took a sharp veer to the right and Sean's body swung left.

"Damn, dude. Your mom is gonna keep the food warm. No rush. We can't eat if we dead."

Damien gave Sean a side-eye mean-mug. "I'll say it again like I've said before. All the muscles in this body are hard to control. Oh, but wait. Your scrawny ass wouldn't know nothin' about that." Damien laughed and now it was Sean who was doing the mean-mugging.

He was right, though. Not about being able to control the muscles, but just the mere fact that his body was quite muscular. Damien had always had an athletic body and he'd always been into keeping up his physical features. His total body fat was only about twelve percent and for some strange reason, people trusted him to train them to have a sexy hot bod just like him. He was one of the most sought after athletic trainers at the fitness center where he worked.

Sean and Damien pulled into Victorian Estates just as one of the twins had. They both parked in the driveway. The two friends gave David dap and a half hug before entering the house.

As soon as they entered, they could smell the aroma floating from the kitchen all around the house. Mom must've put her foot in another pot because all the young men followed an invisible trail to the kitchen while rubbing their stomachs and licking their lips.

"Did I just hear my boys walk in?" Deborah and Donovan were in the dining room setting the table.

They made a detour to the dining room and Damien and David got into a scuffle match to see who would hug their mother first. Damien, with all his muscle mass, won out and grabbed Deborah, spinning her around in the air.

"Hey Mom! It smells delicious in here." Damien gave her a kiss on the cheek before greeting his other brother.

Deborah turned to Sean. "My son from another mom!" She smiled and embraced him and he returned the affection. "It feels like years since I've seen you! How is Cassie? I haven't spoken to her in a couple months."

"Mom is good. I told her I was coming over here for dinner today. She told me to tell you, and I quote, 'Tell that heifer to call me.'" Sean covered his head with his hands and forearms so Mrs. Johnson couldn't slap him over the head for calling her a heifer, even though they technically weren't his words.

Everyone in the room laughed. "Oh, I'm definitely going to call her alright!" Deborah responded in laughter. "Let's go fix these plates, boys!"

All the young men followed Deborah's lead to the kitchen and the feast was finally in full view. She had made a garden salad with tomatoes, purple cabbage, carrots, cucumbers, eggs, shredded Colby Jack cheese, and croutons. The main entrée was spaghetti with Italian sausage and slices of garlic bread. And if anyone had room in their stomachs for dessert, there was banana pudding to top it all off. With four hungry young men, it was about to get real. They would put a dent in that food real quick.

They all prepared their plates and filed back to the dining room. Deborah took her seat first followed by her sons and Sean. They bowed their heads, closed their eyes, and put their hands together to say grace, then proceeded to chow down on the deliciously cooked meal. It wasn't long before the small talk in between chews began.

"So, where's Dad?" Damien directed his question to his mother.

"I don't know. Probably somewhere with his hoe," she answered back.

"Mom…" Damien turned to quickly glance at Sean, silently indicating for her to act civilized in front of their guest.

Sean, on the contrary, was taking it all in stride. He was ready for some shit to pop off.

"Sean ain't nobody. Well, nobody for me to be faking the funk for. But to rephrase my prior statement, your father and I aren't exactly on speaking terms, so I don't know where he is. There, is that better?" Deborah sarcastically asked her eldest son before changing the topic.

"How's Paula?" She made direct eye contact with Sean. He hadn't prepared himself to answer any questions regarding Paula. He immediately regretted that now.

"Umm, she's good, I think." He quickly stuffed a fork full of spaghetti in his mouth, chewing vigorously in order not to speak.

"You think?" Mrs. Johnson questioned. "Don't you live together?" She knew good and well that Sean had been staying at Damien's, but that wasn't going to stop her prodding.

Sean swallowed before answering. "Well, we did. But we had a bit of a falling out."

"Oh, that's too bad. You two were so cute together."

"Oh yeah, I forgot to tell y'all the good news!" Damien purposely interrupted. "Sean and I started a business called Don't Shoot the Messenger." He had already told his brothers about it, but went over the details again so his mother could hear. David and Damien gave them dap for a job well done. Mrs. Johnson didn't have quite the same sentiments.

"That's the silliest thing I've ever heard. Breaking up with people for money. You kids these days—" Deborah shook her head as she took in a mouthful of ranch covered salad.

"Well, I think there are always situations where one person may feel like they've exhausted all other avenues and just no longer want to be bothered. And Mr. Johnson gave us a loan to get started," Sean added.

"Oh, is that so? Of course he didn't share that information with me," Deborah responded to Sean. She continued, "Well, I'm not a fan of the whole idea and I believe anyone who purchases this service is a coward. BUT, I love you boys and wish you the best. Deborah smiled at both Damien and Sean.

"Thanks, Mom."

"Thanks, Mrs. Johnson," Sean responded, trying to sound as non-cowardly as possible.

Chapter Nine

Sean spotted her as she entered through the sliding doors and grabbed a green hand held basket to carry her items in. He was determined to, at the bare minimum, find out what her name was.

He didn't want to seem like a perverted stalker, so he held his post at the customer service counter until he could figure out the right move. As soon as that thought passed, he noticed an elderly woman reaching for some Gain detergent that she couldn't quite grasp from a high shelf. Sean abandoned his area to go give the customer some assistance.

"Good afternoon, ma'am. Allow me to give you a hand."

"Thank you, handsome. You're such a gentleman," her old voice cracked as she spoke and smiled at him.

Just as Sean was placing the detergent in her buggy, Anonymous Woman came strolling around the corner and made direct eye contact with Sean.

He turned back to the old lady. "Have a wonderful day, ma'am."

His focus quickly returned to Anonymous Woman. Time to step his game up.

"You finding everything okay today?"

Anonymous Woman looked at him. "Yes. Thank you."

"Well, if you need anything just let me know. My name is Sean."

"Okay. Thanks Sean."

He knew that if he stayed any longer, he would stare and might start salivating out of the corners of his mouth, so he walked away. He didn't know her name yet, but at least she knew his.

He decided to stroll the aisles then go assist with bagging. That would give him another opportunity to discover Anonymous Woman's real name and possibly get the digits. It was just his luck that the same elderly woman he'd helped with the detergent needed assistance getting to her car as soon as he walked up. At first he thought about delegating the task to someone else; after all, he was the manager on duty. Then on second thought, he figured he might get some brownie points if Anonymous Woman saw him being such a gentleman.

He finished loading Mrs. Tucker's truck with her green recyclable Publix grocery bags. After he called her "ma'am" for the hundredth time, she finally shared her name. It wasn't quite the name of the woman he wanted to learn, but as Sean was closing her driver's side door and waving goodbye, he noticed Anonymous Woman exiting the building carrying three bags in her hands. He saw an open door and decided to walk through.

"You need any help getting to your car, ma'am?" He pleasantly asked.

"No, thanks. I'm good."

"I'm sorry, I didn't catch your name."

"Well, that's because I never threw it, and you never asked," she replied, giving him a smile and a slow shoulder shrug.

"Touché. So, may I have your name so that I may properly address you?"

"The name is Toni."

"Beautiful name for a beautiful woman. So, Toni, may I call you sometime?" Sean boldly asked while still on the clock.

"Is that you asking me for my number?"

"Yes, it is." Sean admitted.

"I'm not really into giving my number out. Sorry," she responded.

"Okay, that's cool. I understand." That's what came out of his mouth, but he knew that if he were Damien, he'd not only have the digits by now, but he'd have the panties, too. He hated comparing himself to Damien, but sometimes he just couldn't help it.

Just as Sean was about to give her his salutations and head back inside, she cut him off.

"But I'll take your number, though."

Sean tried to keep his composure as she pulled her phone out of her fashionable Coach handbag. Sean gave her his ten-digit phone number and made sure she spelled his name the correct way. They parted ways and for the next few days, Sean played the waiting game.

The Don't Shoot the Messenger Facebook page had received a little over three hundred likes, and on Sean's day off, he decided to add to their social media marketing by creating a Twitter and Instagram account as well. As he was in the beginning stages of creating the Twitter account, he received a notification alert on his cell phone. Looking at the notifications bar at the top of the screen, he noticed it was the Facebook message icon.

His heart rate began to increase and moisture began to build in his pores. A small smirk began to appear on his face and the possibilities of who it could be ran across his mind. He and Damien had been excited to get their business off the ground. It was just all a matter of waiting for someone to contact them via Facebook, email, call or text. Could this be their first client?

He wanted to go get Damien out of the room, but he had brought some chick home the night before and Sean hadn't yet heard her creep out. It was a shock that Sean was even awake before double digits on the clock seeing as though the head board banging, moaning, and groaning ran long into the night. He would definitely have to invest in some ear plugs. He didn't mind the sound of sex, but he didn't want to get off from his best friend having sex with some random chick. That was just weird.

Sean thought to hell with it and opened up the message. It was from a female by the Facebook name of Ebony-Loves-Ivory Alexander. Her message read that she had been seeing a guy named Larry for about four months. All of her life, she had always been attracted to white men and she went out with Larry to see what all the fuss was about. After her experience with Larry, she didn't think he deserved a big fuss, let alone a quiet whisper. He was a nice guy, but just not what she was used to or into. His stroke was good, but the chemistry was lacking, which for her, was an important factor. White was definitely alright with her. Her message also indicated that she had tried to gently break it off with her chocolate lover, but he just wasn't taking heed to the hints being given or the big bold writings on the wall. So, when she came across the Facebook page, she figured she'd give it a try.

She left her cell phone number as the best way to reach her and hoped to hear back from Sean or Damien soon. Their business page promised a seventy-two hour turn-around for a response to all inquiries or ten percent off any Don't Shoot the Messenger service. Sean wanted to respond right away, but figured it would be best for Damien to read the message before doing anything.

He got up and banged on Damien's bedroom door like the police looking for America's Most Wanted. He could hear the bed squeak and covers shuffle about as Damien tried to fight his way out of bed and to the door.

He cracked the door ajar just enough for his nose to slide through.

"What the hell do you want? You know I have a fine piece of ass in here," Damien was visibly frustrated as he gritted the words through his teeth trying to camouflage them so his naked guest wouldn't get offended.

"Yeah, I know, but we got business," Sean whispered loudly.

"What business?"

"Don't Shoot the Messenger."

The door slammed in Sean's face and soon after he could hear the chick angrily questioning Damien.

Sean returned to the cushion of the couch which had become his home and tuned to ESPN while he waited. Soon thereafter, the girl stormed out of the room and through the living room to the front door.

"I'll call you!" Damien yelled, pulling his sweatpants up over his navy blue Ralph Lauren boxer briefs.

"Don't bother!" She slammed the door behind her.

"What's up, man?" Damien inquired, taking his usual spot on the couch opposite of Sean.

"We have a message." Sean couldn't help but to reveal some of his teeth as the words slipped out. He passed the laptop over to let Damien read it.

"Oh shit. She likes that white meat," Damien chuckled. Then continued, "So, what's the next move?"

"We call her and set it up," Sean answered.

He dialed the number on the business card and gently placed the phone to his right ear. The phone rang four times before she answered.

"Paula Davis Interior Design. How may I improve your home today?" This was Paula's normal way of answering her business cell phone when the incoming number was from an unknown caller.

"Hi, Ms. Davis. My name is Joseph Hall, and I received your card from Mr. Tim Johnson. I was calling to get some information about the services you offer. I've visited your webpage, and I really like the work I'm seeing."

Paula smiled before replying, "Thank you, Mr. Hall. I'm glad you liked the webpage. As I'm sure you saw, I offer a variety of services. Anywhere from simply organizing your closet to furnishing your home to major renovations. What type of service are you looking for?"

"Well, I just moved into a condo, but I'm having a hard time furnishing it. I could use some assistance.

"Okay. How about we set up a time for me to stop by and get a visual of the space," Paula insisted.

Joe agreed, and they set a date for a meet and greet later that week.

"Christine, has my package arrived yet?" Tim asked over the intercom of his office phone.

"Yes, Mr. Johnson. I'll bring it right now."

About two minutes later, she entered Tim's office through the already slightly opened door. She closed it behind her and turned the lock to prevent anyone else from entering.

Tim stood up behind his desk and walked around it to greet her waist with his firm hands. Their tongues met first, then their lips with passion, and he lifted her, leaving her legs straddling around his body. He grabbed her ass and squeezed her cheeks. Carrying her over to his wooden desk, he gently sat her on top. He began to unbutton her blouse as she returned the favor to his pants. She stroked his penis with her soft hands. He pulled her black bra straps down past her shoulders and tasted her warm plump breasts, one at a time, in his mouth while his tongue moved about around her areola. She quietly moaned with pleasure as he did so. Soon, the sensation was unbearable. Her nipples protruded. In his pants, the laws of gravity were being defied, and the moisture oozing out of her juice box began to seep through her panties. He jerked her down and bent her over the desk, lifting her skirt up in what seemed to be all one steady motion. Tim entered her from behind and in the midst of their sexual encounter, the picture of Deborah and him somehow found its way on the cold, tile floor.

Chapter Ten

Sean waited in the van while Damien waited at the bottom of the staircase. They both had the picture of Larry that Ebony had sent them pulled up on their phones. They were waiting on him to get home from his job at the local Best Buy.

Once Ebony had given Sean all the information he and Damien needed, Larry's address, his schedule, a description of his car, and his picture, they drove the fifteen miles to his apartment complex to deliver the news. Now, they waited.

They agreed that Damien would always be the bearer of bad news and Sean would be on standby as backup and ready to jump in if necessary. But Sean's main job was to connect with all the clients, get their information, set the scene and collect the money. Sean was the assisting point guard and Damien was the scorer. Together they were a two-man dream team.

About thirty minutes passed before the duo saw a car that fit the description of Larry's. A black Toyota Camry with tented windows and a busted left tail light. Yep, that was Larry.

He parked and exited his car with his blue collared work shirt on, making his way toward the direction of his apartment building and towards Damien.

Damien was doing a decent job at keeping his composure from what Sean could see. He, on the other hand, was about to have a nervous breakdown, and he wasn't even a part of the main action.

Damien stood up as Larry approached and extended his right hand to greet him. Sean began to snap photos to show to Ebony as proof of the message being delivered. Damien was supposed to be recording the conversation.

"Hi, are you Larry?" Damien asked, right hand in midair.

"Yes, and you are?" Larry inquired, but accepted the handshake being offered.

"I'm with a company called Don't Shoot the Messenger and I was sent by a female named Ebony Alexander. Do you know her?"

"Yeah, that's my girlfriend. What exactly is Don't Shoot the Messenger?" There was frustration in Larry's voice as he tried to understand what was going on.

"Well, that's just it. She doesn't want to be your girlfriend anymore. She tells us that she has tried to break it off with you, but nothing has worked. So, she sought out our services, which is why I'm here," Damien explained.

"What? Is this some type of joke?"

"Unfortunately, it's not. Ms. Alexander no longer wishes to be your girlfriend, and she does not want to be contacted by you anymore."

"What? Why?" Larry was obviously confused.

"To be quite honest, she's into white guys. Dude, just take my advice and leave her alone. She doesn't want you." Damien was beginning to grow impatient.

"You know what? Fuck you! And fuck that bitch too! I'm seeing somebody else anyway. Go give Ebony that message!" Larry pushed past Damien and stormed up the concrete steps.

"Sure you are," Damien mumbled under his breath as he made his way back to where Sean awaited.

"That looked intense!" Sean exclaimed with excitement.

"He's gonna cry when he gets upstairs."

They both laughed and gave each other a high-five. Their first delivery was complete and now it was time to collect the payment.

Ebony had been on standby until the mission was complete. She waited nearby to meet Sean and Damien so she could hear audio and see the pictures. Once she was satisfied with what she saw and heard, she signed the dotted line and made her payment in cash. She also promised to hashtag Don't Shoot the Messenger on all her social media profiles.

First-time jitters were gone and Sean and Damien gloated as they made their first successful delivery. They were confident that as time passed, their number of inquiries and deliveries would increase and a profit would soon start to form.

As the moon and stars settled into place, so did Sean on the couch. He had a shift at Publix bright and early the next morning. Just as his eyes were closing, he heard his phone beep. It could have been a notification for many things, so he picked it up to check. It could be another potential client. He slid his right thumb across the screen of his Samsung in a triangular motion. The circles lit up with a green outline and his phone was unlocked and ready for use. The notification was that of a text, but the number was not a familiar one. He opened up the message to read it in its entirety and grinned at the sight of the name Toni.

The conversation began by text, but after an hour of swiping his finger across the letters of the touch-screen phone, Sean decided to call Toni. His thumb was tired of texting and he wanted to hear the sound of her voice. When he called, they spoke for hours, just like two teenagers. They talked about all their favorites: colors, flavor of ice cream, movies, songs, foods, hobbies. They even shared all of their biggest dreams: dream careers, dream cars, dream homes. When they finally hung up after hours of stimulating conversation, it was almost three in the morning.

Sean lay there, his heart and body filled with exhilaration. He felt like a kid again. He felt the way he did ten years ago when he and Paula had started talking. Their relationship began in a similar manner, minus the texting. He and Paula used to spend hours on the phone, sometimes talking about nothing, and sometimes just listening to each other breathe. He wondered what would happen with him and Toni. Then he wondered if Paula had met someone else. But he couldn't let those thoughts consume his mind. He was happy that he'd finally spoken to his Publix crush, and things were starting to look up.

There was no doorbell, so Paula knocked on the door five times, one consistently behind the other. She could smell the fresh scent of Warm Vanilla Sugar hand lotion purchased from Bath and Body Works that she had just applied before getting out of the car.

She heard the deadbolt unlock and began to get excited about meeting a new client. A new client meant new money. She was wearing a full smile when the door completely opened.

"Hi, I'm Paula," she grinned and held her hand out to greet Joe.

He stared her up and down, noticing her black heels, dark blue form-fitting jeans, white button-up, and black blazer before taking her silky smooth hand in his. "Hi, Paula. I'm Joe. Please, come in." He was mesmerized by her beauty. Her brown mahogany skin was steaming like hot mocha. "It's nice to finally meet you."

"You as well. Your place looks great!" She noticed the dark hardwood flooring that flowed throughout, the updated kitchen with quartz counters and plenty of cabinet space. She loved the open and airy feeling that the condo gave off, and the massive window in the living room let in all the natural light that anyone could ever ask for.

"Thank you. I love it so far, except of course my lack of furniture as I'm sure you've noticed."

He was right. There was an extreme lack of furniture. But that's why Paula was there, to change that.

"Well, Paula has come to your rescue." As Paula spoke in the third person, they met eyes, her brown with his blue, and seconds seemed to slow down to minutes. When the momentary trance ended, Joe gave Paula a tour of his home. She questioned him about his style and color preferences and he shared with her what he could. He admitted that during his eleven year marriage, his ex-wife handled a majority of the interior matters and he usually just went with it. He did know, however, that he didn't want any furniture or colors that reminded him of his ex-wife and the home they shared. He was a bachelor now, and he wanted his interior design to speak the same language.

Paula expressed her understanding and promised not to let him down. She knew all too well how it felt to not want to be reminded of an ex, which was why she wanted to move. There were too many memories of her and Sean in the apartment, and she wanted nothing but to move out and start fresh.

"I'm sorry. I'm talking a little bit too much about my personal life," Paula apologized to Joe for turning business into personal.

"It's okay. I could listen to you talk all day."

Paula looked up about seven inches from her 5'4" frame to his 5'11" one and returned the smile that Joe was giving her. He was totally flirting with her!

"Well," she cleared her throat, "I'd better get going so I can hurry up and get this place exquisitely furnished." She began making her way back to the front door, and Joe followed closely behind. He opened the door for her as she spun around to say her last words.

"I will be in touch."

"Please do."

With that, their first meeting concluded. Paula could hear the door shut softly as she strolled down the hall, back to the elevator that had originally lifted her the three stories to Joe's condo.

The next delivery for Don't Shoot the Messenger was scheduled for a week later. Aaron was trying to get rid of his bug-a-boo Kim. He claimed that he had already told her he didn't want her anymore, but she was whipped and wouldn't take no for an answer. He was a one-Don't Shoot the Messenger-step away from putting a restraining order on her ass. He needed the services of Sean and Damien immediately.

On their way to meet Aaron, Sean and Damien had a quick discussion about how they thought the delivery would pan out.

"Aaron made her out to be crazy. How do you think she's gonna take the message?" Sean asked.

"I don't know, but I have a plan if she starts acting crazy."

Ten minutes later, they were parallel parking in front of an old rundown house with an even more rundown Buick with a flat tire sitting in the driveway.

"Damn. This looks like my grandma's house," Sean laughed.

Damien chuckled. "Alright, get the camera ready."

Damien got out of the van and walked past the dried out, brown grass and patches of dirt in the yard. He strolled up the three steps and knocked on the brown wooden door. He turned his recorder on and waited about two minutes before an old lady looking like Cicely Tyson reluctantly opened the door.

"Who you here for, Kim or Keisha?" she glared at him through her glasses sitting on top of her nose with her head titled down.

"Umm, hi. Is Kim available?" Damien asked with a puzzled expression on his face.

She turned around and yelled as loud as she could with her frail voice. "Kim, I told you I didn't want no more hoodlums knocking on my door!"

Damien's left eyebrow raised in shock. He wasn't a hoodlum and he didn't look like one either. The nerve of that old lady! He could hear Kim's voice getting closer in proximity to the door.

"I told Aaron not to –" she stopped mid-sentence when it wasn't Aaron she saw at the door. "Who are you?" Her right hand met her right hip while her left hand stayed intertwined in her hair. From what Damien could tell, it looked like she was taking out her braids. A little baby boy in an all-white onesie came crawling up behind her and grabbed her leg. He lifted himself up into a standing position and then outstretched his arms for Kim to pick him up and straddle him on her hip. She didn't budge.

"Kayla! Come get your brother!" she yelled.

A little girl who looked to be about five came running out and grabbed the baby boy. His cries could be heard as the girl took him into a back room and closed the door.

"Hi. Are you Kim?" Damien held out his right hand.

Kim saw his hand hanging there, then rolled her eyes back up to his face without offering her hand in return.

Damien looked blankly at his hand then let it fall back down to his side.

"My name is Damien. I'm with a company called Don't Shoot the Messenger. Do you know a gentleman by the name of Aaron?"

"I wouldn't call him a gentleman, but yeah, I do. And what the hell is Don't Shoot the Messenger?"

"Well, ma'am, we are a break-up service. Aaron has expressed that he no longer wants to be your boyfriend and that he's told you several times, but you refuse to leave him alone."

Her look of confusion turned into bewilderment.

"Oh, hell no! He's the one who's always coming over here trying to get some of this cookie! But that's alright 'cause I got something for his ass!"

Sean held in his laughter as he snapped photos from a short distance away. With the windows partially rolled down, he could hear her loud shrieks of anger.

"I know you're upset, but this is not a bad thing."

Kim rolled her eyes.

"I just met Aaron, but from what I've seen, he's a loser. He talked down about you. I'm sure he's not ready to raise another man's children. And he told us he's seeing somebody else. I know you must want more for yourself and for your family. Just leave him alone. He couldn't even be a man and tell you all this himself." There was a momentary silence. "Am I right?"

She paused before responding. "Yeah, you right. I can do better than his ass."

"Then you should. Don't chase behind no man who doesn't want you," Damien added.

"You don't know me, okay? So stop talking to me like you do. You only know a little bit about a little bit, which really ain't nothing at all."

"I'm just trying to help," Damien pleaded his case.

"But if he wants it to be over, it can be over, but only when I say so," Kim spoke very matter-of-factly.

"Here." Damien reached in his pocket and grabbed a business card out of his wallet. "Take this. If you feel like you want to call him or see him, just call me and I'll try to persuade you not to because you deserve better."

"Thanks, but no thanks. I can handle myself. Can I help you with anything else?" The one hand was no longer in her hair, but the other one was still on her hip.

"No, ma'am. Have a good day."

He could barely get "day" out before she slammed the door in his face. He wasn't even mad. He knew with the business he and Sean were now in, there would be plenty more of those. He hoped his words would marinate in her mind and that she really would leave Aaron alone. He just had a feeling that Aaron was a real asshole and that she was really not who she appeared to be on the outside. He placed the business card down on the ground in front of the door and crept back to the van where Sean awaited.

"That looked interesting," Sean said with a smirk on his face.

"She wasn't that bad. What the hell are you smiling at?"

"She looked like she was about to pounce on you at one point. Lay those paws on you!" Sean laughed.

"Oh, you mean like Paula?"

That pumped the brakes on Sean's laughter real quick.

"Damn, I'm just having a little fun. No need for personal low blows."

"I'm just saying," Damien said with a straight face. "So where are we meeting Aaron?"

"Back at his job," Sean responded in an extremely stale voice.

They rode in silence for about fifteen minutes before pulling up at a Big and Tall clothing store. Sean called Aaron to come meet them outside and three minutes later he was getting into the van. From the outside looking in, it looked like a drug deal was about to go down.

Sean showed him the pictures and Damien played the audio. Aaron listened to the entire audio before expressing his satisfaction, or lack thereof.

"Y'all are pretty good." Aaron complimented.

"Thanks," Sean accepted the compliment on both his and Damien's behalf.

"Using a break-up service to pick up chicks. That's genius. You just tried to holler at my girl. What's that shit about?" Aaron directed his dissatisfaction towards Damien.

"Your girl?" Damien questioned. "One, ain't nobody trying to holler at nobody. If I wanted to get with her, please believe it would happen. Two, how is she your girl when you're paying us to break up with her?"

"I'm not paying y'all shit! Y'all services sucked. She clearly still doesn't get it, and I'm not paying y'all jack cause I know she'll be blowing up my phone later." Aaron started to exit the van.

"I don't know where the hell you think you're going without paying us!" Damien followed him out the van and through the parking lot. Sean quickly followed in their footsteps.

"I already told y'all I'm not paying. Now if y'all wanna cross this threshold, there's a couple big and tall dudes in the back that I'm sure wouldn't mind getting their knuckles dirty." Aaron's right fist hit his left palm as a seal to the promise he'd just made.

Sean grabbed Damien's shoulder. "It ain't even worth it."

Damien wasn't one to back down from a fight, but he knew this was one that he probably wouldn't win. He slowly made his way back to the van, smiling at the simple fact that if Aaron had've been by himself, he would've beat his ass.

Paula searched around Ikea on a hunt to find nice furnishings for Joe's condo. She sent him a few picture messages to get his opinion on some colors and patterns for the living room.

He received her picture messages just as he was entering the financial services building where Tim worked.

"Hi. I'm here to see Tim."

Christine buzzed Tim's office and then led Joe to the door.

"Hi, Joe." Tim stood up from behind his desk and greeted Joe with a firm handshake. "Thank you for meeting with me today."

"No problem. Has there been a change in the budget we set?" Joe questioned Tim.

"No. My request for you to meet me actually has nothing to do with your budget," Tim admitted.

"Oh?" Joe wore a puzzled expression on his face.

"I called you here because I need a personal favor."

Chapter Eleven

After the whole fiasco with Aaron, Sean and Damien had to reevaluate the structure of their business. Basically, folks had to fill out the paperwork, provide certain documentation and pay up front. They changed the language in the contract to match their new requirements.

One of the biggest changes was the way in which they would accept payments. Clients would now have to put down a deposit for the full amount of services up front. If the delivery went as planned, the deposit would be their payment. If, on the other hand, the client and the company agreed that the delivery did not go well, then half of the deposit would be non-refundable and the other half would be returned to the client. Under no circumstance would a full refund be given and under no circumstance would services be rendered until payment was made. Clients could also now pay with a debit or credit card. Sean purchased a portable debit and credit swiper that could be attached to his phone. For a mobile business like theirs, a device like that was much needed. Sean also made sure to update all of their social media cites. They were now ready for business, again.

Sean finally had a day off from both Publix and Don't Shoot the Messenger, so he took care of printing out the new contracts. He was excited about the new changes they had made. He knew those changes would be beneficial to the company in the long run. He was even more excited, though, for the plans he'd made with Toni for later that night. They'd planned on going roller skating on a double-date with Damien and his overnight chick. He figured they must've made up from the morning he sent her packing without any notice.

Just like a kid in high school again, discovering puppy love for the first time, Sean was going to go home, model some clothes until he found his best outfit, and do anything he could to make eight o'clock arrive as quickly as possible.

Paula arrived with a car load full of knick-knacks and household items to clothe Joe's naked condo just as the Ikea truck was pulling up with the large pieces of furniture.

Ikea was one of Paula's favorite places to shop. They had the type of modern and eccentric furniture that she adored, and she loved mixing and matching different pieces together. She couldn't wait to decorate Joe's place. He had provided her with a hefty budget and she was confident that he'd be amazed at the transformation that was about to take place.

She packed her four wheel dolly with as much as she could and led the delivery men up to Joe's condo. Joe opened the door with wide eyes, surprised to see Paula and the delivery men all at once.

"Looks like perfect timing! Come on in." Joe stepped to the side, still holding the door open for everyone to enter.

The delivery men started with the living room furniture: an ivory fabric two-piece sectional sofa with a matching chaise lounge chair, gray coffee and end tables with glass surfaces, and distinguished lamps to go atop the end tables.

Paula, in an effort to not get in the way of the movers, began with the bathroom. She decorated the guest bath with tan and multiple shades of green. The shower curtain was a checkerboard of green squares while the three rugs were tan. Two palm tree pictures covered the walls. Two candles and a bowl of pebble rocks rested on the countertops. Decorative matching towels were hung to complete the space.

The day went about in a similar manner; the Ikea men traveled from space to space putting furniture together and Paula went wherever they weren't. Joe had to step out to make a court appearance, but promised he'd be back in a few hours. Paula didn't mind that he'd be gone. She didn't like for her clients to be home the entire time while she worked. It took away from the element of surprise, and that was the best part.

Paula unboxed dishes, pots, pans, silverware, a knife set and all other things belonging in the kitchen. Paula liked to take her time and have everything just so. An hour passed before the kitchen was complete. While the furniture men put the last few pieces together in the bedrooms, Paula decorated the living room and added a large abstract painting to the wall. Then she went downstairs to get the remaining items that waited to be arranged in their new home.

When the Ikea employees finally finished putting the bedroom furniture together, Paula signed the paperwork. All the furniture had been delivered, put together, and there were no damages. The only thing left to decorate were the two bedrooms. She began with the guest bedroom. There wasn't much to do other than make the bed, hang a picture on the wall, and put a glass vase filled with ocean breeze scented potpourri in the center of the dresser. That room, as Joe had shared with her, was going to be for his daughter when she came to visit.

When Paula finally arrived to Joe's master suite, there was a little more work to do. She began with the black and red comforter and sheet set. She topped the bed off with three decorative pillows. One circular solid black, one squared solid red, and the last rectangular one a combination of the two colors with a circled design covering the front. She placed a black arm chair delivered from Ikea in one of the corners facing the bed.

The red and black continued into the bathroom. But just as she was placing the rugs down on the floor, she heard a bang. She ran to the front door to discover that the banging noise she'd heard was caused by the chain lock on the door. Joe was back. Paula forgot that she had put the chain on after the furniture men left. When Joe got back home, she wanted to be able to keep the element of surprise that she loved so much.

"I'm sorry. I just wanted to surprise you," Paula explained to Joe through the small opening of the door.

"It's okay. I actually wanted to do the same," Joe smiled at her.

"Oh." Paula was shocked. Talk about being surprised.

"How about this? You step out here and I give you your surprise first," Joe suggested.

Paula concurred, saying, "Okay," and took the chain off the door. She stepped into the hallway and was greeted by Joe with a bouquet of red roses and a huge, over-sized Hershey's kiss. Her eyes lit up at the sight.

"This is just a little something to show my appreciation of all your time and hard work," Joe smiled at her.

"Aww. You didn't have to do this! It's only right that I put in a lot of time and hard work. That's what you paid me to do." She was beginning to blush and she could feel her cheeks turning the same rosy red color as the flowers she was now holding in her hand.

"I know I didn't have to, but I wanted to," Joe said to her with a grin on his face.

"Thank you." Paula finally succumbed to his generosity.

"Okay, your turn, or my turn. I'm not quite sure how to phrase it. Your turn to surprise me," Joe smiled.

Paula laughed and quickly went inside to place her flowers and candy on the kitchen counter top. She came back out and stood behind Joe, placing each one of her hands over each of his eyes, and led him inside.

"Voila!" Paula exclaimed with excitement. "I have renamed this The Diner," Paula told Joe as she removed the makeshift blindfold that she had created with her hands.

"Wow. Now when I have a special guest over for dinner, I can prepare her meal and serve it on a real plate and with fine silverware." He looked down at her to indicate that he was talking about her.

Paula had never gone out with an older gentleman, let alone a white one. She was, however, greatly attracted to not only his physicality, but to his personality as well. Momentarily though, she ignored his subtle advances and moved on to the next room.

"This is The Relaxer. You can come here to relax on your new couch and watch some TV." Paula held her hand out like she was a model on The Price is Right. "Take a seat."

"Only if you sit with me."

There was a slight hesitation, but it didn't last long. She took a seat next to Joe on the couch and they admired the new painting on the wall.

"Okay, let's go. There are a few more rooms to see."

Paula led the way to the guest bathroom.

"This is The Jungle. Green was your second favorite color on the list, so here it is."

"Nice. I like the shower curtain design."

"Good. Moving on to The Guest Room," Paula said as she took a few steps down the hall.

"Mandy will love having her own space when she comes to visit. I hope she likes the living room better though. I miss her," Joe said gazing in the room as if he could see his daughter in there at that moment.

"I'm sure she misses her daddy, too," Paula said reassuringly. "Shall we?" Paula asked pointing to the master suite.

"You take the lead."

Paula took a few more steps and arrived to Joe's room.

"And now, saving the best for last, we've finally arrived to The King's Corner!"

Joe stepped inside and did a panorama of the room. He was amazed at how such minimal changes, or what seemed to be pretty minimal, could make such a significant difference in the display and feel of a room. He continued in the bathroom while Paula waited in the room. He still hadn't said anything, and she was starting to get nervous.

"Now this is a real king's corner," he said to Paula as he came back into the bedroom."

"So, you like it?" Paula asked.

"What's not to like?" Joe questioned.

"Well, nothing I hope."

"I like the furniture and design, and I especially like the person who put it together." Joe took a step closer to Paula and they glared in each other's eyes.

Joe leaned in for a kiss on Paula's full lips, and initially, she resisted. But he leaned in again and this time there was no resisting. Their lips came together with intense passion. They both longed for love, for the soft caress from the opposite sex. Joe was unhappy about his divorce; it was something he thought he'd never go through. And Paula was still hurt from the break-up with Sean. They needed each other, even if it wasn't real, even if it wouldn't last past that night.

He undressed her and laid her down on the new red and black comforter. The soft linens beneath her gave her comfort and relaxed her tense muscles. He lifted her legs and lowered his head between the mounds of her caramel thighs. She moaned with pleasure and grabbed his hair with her left hand while the other was straddled above her head.

Joe momentarily stopped pleasuring Paula and made his way to the bathroom under the sink. He was in search of a little box he'd received from his younger, single brother as a divorce gift. Once he located the box, he reached inside for what he was looking for and returned to the damsel whom awaited.

He undid his belt, unzipped his pants and let them drop to the floor. Then he opened the Trojan package and slid the condom onto his protruding penis. He got on top of Paula. Missionary. He kept it simple. Just the feel of their bodies touching was enough seduction for the both of them. It wasn't long before they both climaxed. They inhaled and exhaled heavily and shared another wet and passionate kiss.

That night, they fell asleep in each other's arms.

Sean and Toni agreed to meet each other at the skating rink. Damien hadn't been home all day. He and his overnight chick spent the afternoon together and they would meet Toni and Sean at the skating rink as well. Sean figured Damien must've been trying to make up for the morning he put her out spur of the moment.

When Sean finally figured out what he would wear – army fatigue shorts, a candy red shirt with the word #COOL in black letters across his chest, and his red, black and white Jordan 11's – he decided to leave home early so he could make a pit stop at the gas station. Plus, he wanted to beat Toni there. The last thing he wanted was for her to be waiting on him. That wouldn't make for a good first impression on a first date.

After he filled up his tank, he drove straight to Smooth Wheels skating rink. More adults were beginning to arrive at the same time. Sunday night was reserved for skaters eighteen and over to get their roll bounce on.

Toni arrived about twenty minutes later. She texted Sean as she parked and soon thereafter he came out to meet her in the parking lot. They hugged at the sight of seeing each other again, and Sean slipped his arm around her neck as they strolled inside the building. Sean had already paid her way, so the only thing she had to do was trade her shoes for roller skates.

"They've been playing some jams!" Sean spoke loudly so Toni could hear him over the music.

"I haven't been here in a couple years, but when my dad used to bring me as a little girl, the music was always on point!" Toni replied.

Just as the words rolled off her tongue, one of the greatest roller skating songs in history was about to make its debut to begin the night with an introduction from the DJ.

"Ladies and gentlemen, let's get this skate party started! The kids are gone and it's time to get this skate party going on! We're gonna start this thing off right with a jam I know everybody can roll to. Tie those laces tight, spin those wheels and get to…" Just then the Vaughan Mason and Crew classic disco song began to play, "Bounce, Rock, Skate, Roll".

Both Sean and Toni's eyes glowed with excitement at the sound of those opening lyrics. They hopped up off the bench they were sitting on to tie their laces. They skated slowly across the carpet to the slick skating floor and both had minor trouble at first keeping their balance. Neither of them had been skating in at least two years. But after a few strokes of their feet, they were finally in rhythm and in sync with the song and each other. Skating is just like riding a bike. People don't forget how to skate; they just become a little rusty and out of practice. Eventually, the skill comes back like it was never gone to begin with.

Sean and Toni continued to skate side-by-side while the DJ busted out more hot tunes. Johnny Kemp's "Just Got Paid", Cameo's "Candy", Kool Moe Dee's "I Go to Work", and Montel Jordan's "This Is How We Do It" were the next songs on the DJ's spin list.

As the couple was bending a corner and facing the entrance, Sean spotted Damien and his date finally walking through the door. Sean prompted Toni to exit the skating floor so they could go meet the newly arrived couple.

Sean hated using the actual brakes on his skates, so he skated right into the carpeted curb that separated the skating and walking areas. As a younger kid, every time he tried to use the brake on his skates, he would press on it too abruptly and bust his butt. After some sore tail bones, wrists, and elbows, he finally gave up on the brakes. Then he noticed Toni using her brakes ever so majestically and her smooth transition from the skating floor to the carpet.

"What was that?" she asked after watching his lack of use of his brakes.

"What was what?" Sean purposely looked confused.

Toni shook her head and added, "Never mind."

Sean held out his hand to take hers in his so they could meet Damien and his date halfway. But about halfway to meeting them halfway, Sean realized that he didn't recognize the girl Damien was with. She wasn't overnight chick.

The best friends gave each other dap upon approaching and made their introductions. Then Damien and his date, Vanessa, went to go rent their roller skates while Toni and Sean slowly rolled across the carpet to grab a whole pizza pie, wings, and drinks. They found an empty table to sit down and enjoy their food. As they devoured the greasy, thin crust pepperoni pizza, they noticed Damien escorting Vanessa around the large circular skating floor. She could barely maneuver her legs back and forth without losing her balance, which required Damien to have to hold her up. They made it around twice, which was equivalent to one song, before she quit and came to plop herself down at the table with Sean and Toni.

"I totally suck at this!" Vanessa said looking at Toni.

Toni smiled and replied, "Practice makes perfect. Is this your first time?"

"No. It's my second." Both ladies burst out in laughter. "I went to a friend's birthday party in the fourth grade and it was the most embarrassing day of my life."

Sean used the opportunity of the ladies talking to escape back to the skating floor to join Damien. Sean entered on a curve, but Damien was already on the next straightaway, so Sean picked up speed, skating in long strides, to catch up. He strolled up right behind Damien and tried to pants him, but he had a belt on. Damien's reflexes made him grip his pants, but when he realized what was happening, he took a swing at Sean but missed merely inches away from his face.

"I should knock yo' ass out!" Damien yelled, speeding up his pace to catch up to Sean who had now skated past him.

"Yeah, if you can catch me!" Sean teased like a little kid.

They played a game of cat and mouse for a few minutes and that ended with them huffing and puffing, dropping themselves down on a nearby bench.

"So, I thought you were bringing ol' girl who spent the night. What happened to her?" Sean questioned Damien after catching his breath.

"Man, she's trying to be my girl. She wanna come over all the time and be spitting that Steve Harvey shit to me. You know I'm not with that. I had to move on to the next one. Hit it and quit it! You know me," Damien laughed, nudging Sean's arm.

Sean smiled. "Boy, you a fool, but play on playa."

"And you know this…"

"Man!" they both finished the Smokey quote in unison.

"So, what's going on with this Toni chick? I know you're not trying to start a relationship with her," Damien stared at Sean with piercing eyes.

"What are you talking about? We're just hanging out and having fun."

"Yeah, yeah," Damien was unconvinced. "You still love Paula anyway, but have fun with Toni in the meantime. Make sure you at least hit it before you go running back," Damien said laughing.

Sean was in no mood to talk to Damien about love because it was a topic he knew nothing about. So he smacked him upside his big head instead. That was all she wrote. They were back at it, Damien chasing Sean around the skating rink. They made a full 360° around, but Sean bent the next corner with a little too much juice. His front wheels caught the back of another skater, and Sean went airborne before his body slammed into the slippery wood with a shrieking crack that was later determined to be a fractured left forearm.

The loud *thump* got everyone's attention. Toni hurried to Sean's aid, behind Damien, and Vanessa tried to inch her way to the scene as best she could without causing another scene of her own. Double-date night had abruptly come to an end.

Paula was awakened suddenly by the sound of chirping birds singing their sweet morning melodies. When she realized it was the next morning, her mind began to race at the thought of what had transpired the night before. She looked to her right to see Joe still sleeping peacefully. She slipped out of bed with minimal movement and in a quiet rush put her clothes on. Making sure she left none of her personals behind, she tiptoed her way to the front door, leaving it unlocked as she quietly closed it behind her.

Chapter Twelve

5 Months Later

"About time you showed up. I'm on my second glass of wine," Cassie said to Deborah as she took a seat at the small squared table.

"Girl, I'm sorry. This case I'm working on at work is taking up so much of my time." Deborah removed her blazer before taking a seat.

"Uh-huh." I feel like I haven't seen you in forever! You look good!" Cassie complimented Deb.

"It has been forever! I've missed my friend!" Deb outstretched both arms and the ladies tightly embraced.

"So, what's been going on in the Johnson household?" Cassie inquired. "You and Tim still at odds?"

"At odds? Girl, you mean at each other's throats! We don't even sleep in the same room anymore. I had to put his ass out! And the boys…they're so stuck up his ass that they think I'm crazy to believe he's been cheating."

Cassie shook her head from side to side. "Deb, I am so sorry to hear this. I just knew you and Tim would be together for forever and always. You and the boys were always his top priority."

"Yeah, well, I guess his priorities have changed," Deborah replied staring down at her menu. "Anyway, how is Harold?"

"He's fine. He got home from work early today, so he's probably prancing around the house naked," Cassie laughed.

"Can I start you off with something to drink, ma'am?" the waiter asked Deborah.

"I'll just have some water. Thank you." The waiter nodded and went to go retrieve Deborah's drink request. She turned her attention back to Cassie. "I can't remember the last time I got home early from work," Deborah shook her head as she spoke.

"Well, I sure hope things at work are going a lot better than things at home. You've got to have some good to balance with the bad," Cassie suggested.

"Work, though, has been rather interesting lately."

"Interesting how?" Cassie questioned, taking another sip of wine.

"There's a new guy. Handsome. Around forty. He's been doing little things like asking me questions about myself and my family. Asking about different little things that I like. Taking selfies with me at the staff party a few weeks ago. Even had one of those fruit baskets delivered to my office." Cassie's eyes were stretching and her eyebrows were raising. "I know it had to be from him even though the card didn't have his name on it. If I didn't know any better, I'd think he was flirting with me." Deb grinned. "I won't stop him, though. I think it's flattering. The attention feels good."

Cassie took yet another sip of wine before responding. "Well, just be careful."

The twosome shared a lunch together while sharing more personal information about what was going on in their lives before eventually parting ways.

"Hello?" Joe answered his phone as he slipped inside his office and closed the door.

"Joe, my man. How are things on your end?"

"Tim. Nice to hear from you. You'll be happy to know that everything is going to plan."

"Good. That's what I like to hear. She'll never know what hit her."

Tim hung up the phone and shared a mighty laugh and zealous kiss with Christine before taking her to lunch.

Chapter Thirteen

Don't Shoot the Messenger had seen a major boost in business in the last few months. They were making up to three deliveries in one day. Sean had significantly cut back on his hours at Publix, and Damien had begun to schedule his workout sessions in between deliveries. Sean had even moved into his own one bedroom apartment, right after he got the cast off his arm. The lease he had shared with Paula finally expired, and he was able to use his funds towards his own place. Damien was happy to see him go. Working and living together was becoming a nuisance. As a company though, they worked well together and were slowly on a rise. They'd even had a few deliveries that involved the moving of furniture and clothing, and they had another one that day.

"So, who are we helping today?" Damien asked.

"We're helping Allison. She says she and her and boyfriend, Mark, dated for two months before she moved in with him. After the first three weeks, he made her quit her job to stay at home. That was four months ago. She's been pregnant, but miscarried. She says that she's tired of Mark controlling her and she wants out."

"Okay. And she has furniture?" Damien questioned more.

"From what she told me, no furniture, just clothes and little house stuff here and there. But she's supposed to be all packed up by the time we get there."

"Good. Let's make this money."

When they arrived to pick Allison up an hour later, she was waiting at the door with eight boxes stacked and ready to be taken to the van. As the contract stated, there were extra fees involved when the business had to assist a client in moving, and the client must have prior arrangements on the location of their new residence, whether temporary or permanent. Allison was going to stay with one of her good friends.

"Thank you guys so much," Allison said to Sean and Damien as they each grabbed two boxes.

"That's what we're here for," Sean smiled reassuringly.

"Mark is going to be here in about two hours," Allison said as she turned her head to look in each direction, as if to check and see if Mark would pull up earlier than expected. He'd done that before – come home early unannounced to see if Allison was up to no good like he always accused her of being. She wasn't messing around; it was his own paranoia.

"Alright. Well let's get you out of here," Damien said as he and Sean carried the last four boxes to the van with Allison following in their footsteps.

She gave Sean the address to her friend's house and he put it in his GPS. Google Maps gave them the quickest route to their destination which would take an estimated twenty one minutes. Sean put the van in gear and they were off.

Once they arrived, Sean and Damien unloaded the boxes and carefully placed them in front of Allison's friend's house. They then headed back to meet the highly anticipated Mark.

When they got back, they had a little time to spare before Mark's arrival.

"I miss her," Sean blurted out of nowhere.

"What?" Damien asked as if he hadn't heard what Sean said the first time, but he did, loud and clear.

"I miss her. Paula." Sean said with his head leaned back against the black headrest, looking at the roof of the van.

"Come on, man. Don't start with that shit," Damien said shaking his head.

"Why can't I just talk about her without you talking shit?" Sean demanded, lifting his head and turning to face Damien.

"Because for months, all that came out of your mouth was how you wanted to break up with her and explore other options. Now that you've broken up and your lease has finally ended and you're totally free, you got your panties up your ass again," Damien snapped back.

"We were together for ten fucking years! It ain't like I'm blowing up her phone. I thought I could talk to you in confidence, but I see I'ma have to keep some shit to myself."

"You may as well call her as much as you talk about her ass. And you – shit!"

Damien was suddenly cut off by the sight of Mark's red, beat up, convertible 1997 Mustang. Feeling unprepared, Damien tried his best to gather his thoughts before exiting the van. He got out simultaneously as Mark got out of his car.

"Mr. Hogan. Mr. Hogan! May I have a word?"

Mark turned around with a look of surprise on his face. "Do I know you?" He sized Damien up and down.

"No, sir, you don't. I am with a business called Don't Shoot the Messenger, and I was sent here by Allison. She no longer wants to be with you and has, in fact, exited the premises of your apartment. She has also changed her number and no longer wishes to have contact with you."

Having gotten used to a number of different reactions, Damien could look in Mark's eyes and tell he was not going to take this delivery very well.

"You wanna run that by me again, boy!" Mark spit in the grass, a brown slimy substance exiting his mouth.

"Which part? The part when I said Allison doesn't want to be with you, she moved out, or she changed her number? And you're looking at all man. No *boy* here," Damien said in a serious tone.

Mark dialed Allison's number, but the woman's voice in the receiver was not Allison's. It was an automated voice to let the caller know that the number was no longer in service. He stormed into his first floor apartment and bum-rushed every square inch. He could tell her things were gone. He dialed another number before going back outside.

"Get over here, now," he spoke into the receiver before hanging up.

Damien had begun to leisurely make his way back to the van, but Mark's words put a halt to his footsteps.

"Hold on there, boy. We ain't done here yet."

Damien stopped in his tracks and then turned around nonchalantly.

"So is Allison a nigger lover now? She in that van of yours you 'bout to get in? Tell that bitch to come out and tell me herself that she don't wanna be with me," Mark demanded.

Damien tried to keep his cool, but the struggle was real.

"If Allison were here, you'd probably try to beat her ass 'cause beating women probably makes you feel like a man and all." Damien walked up close, real close, to Mark's face. "But if you ask me, you're the real boy."

He had put so much emphasis on the b in boy that a little spit came out of his mouth and landed on Mark's forehead. As he wiped the thin film of saliva away, a white pickup truck pulled up and two white men, favoring Mark, got out and slowly walked up to the scene

"Hey boys! Y'all are just in time to meet Allison's new nigger friend here," Mark said looking at Damien.

"Oh, these are boys too? Looks like you're in good company," Damien sarcastically said to Mark, impatiently awaiting his reaction.

Mark just smiled and said, "Who's the nigger lover in your family? Your momma or your daddy?"

It was at that very instant that Damien had lost all patience with the boy and nigger talk. Those were already fighting words, but then to add his parents to the mix made it even worse. Damien's balled up right fist caught Mark in the face right smack dab in the middle of his left cheek. At the sight of that, the other two wasted no time throwing their fists into Damien's body. He could hold his own, but what kind of friend would Sean be if he didn't jump in to help? Despite his bitterness towards Damien at the moment, he hopped out of the van and ran to Damien's aid. He threw a few punches and even inserted a few kicks in the mix. One of Mark's sidekicks was out for the count, making it an even two-on-two, which really wasn't even at all. The brawl would have continued a little longer, but the sirens that they could hear getting closer in proximity brought it to a screeching halt. Sean and Damien both got one more punch in and then ran back to the van. As Sean quickly steered the van out of the complex, they passed right by the police car looking for the scene of the fight. Mark and his boys scurried into the apartment. They already had a warrant, or two, and didn't want any extra trouble with the police. Sean and Damien headed home wiping the trickles of sweat off their foreheads and both breathing a sigh of relief.

Chapter Fourteen

Even though Paula and Joe were technically not in a committed relationship, they were still knockin' the boots every chance they got, which was about every other day. She made him feel young and spontaneous again, and he made her feel…well…wanted again. After the first night they were together and she'd snuck out that next morning, she tried with every ounce in her soul to avoid Joe. It worked for about two weeks, but he was just too consistent and persistent, and she finally surrendered to his pursuit.

They were meeting that day for a short rendezvous and the sweet taste of ice cream at Icy Pleasures. They ordered a triple scoop of French vanilla ice cream with caramel dripping over the top, crunchy pecans, and two large waffle cones that poked out on both sides. Paula grabbed the napkins and Joe grabbed two long white spoons, and they went to sit at a small round table right next to a large, clear window. It was a beautiful day out, but still a little too hot to eat their ice cream outside, unless they wanted it to turn into a warm milkshake.

"So, how was your day?" Joe asked Paula.

She inhaled and let out a heavy breath before responding. "This couple I'm working with now, the Millers, is really annoying."

"What's the problem?"

"I don't even know why they hired me. The wife undermines everything I say and do, and the husband has absolutely no say so at all about anything. I'm ready for this job to be over. But they're wealthy, so I'll be happy to take their money." They both shared a laugh before dipping their spoons into the cold ice cream.

"So, how about you? How was your day?"

"Well, I am currently wrapping up a case I've been working on for a while. I think my client will be highly pleased with the outcome." Joe smiled, taking a bite out of his waffle cone.

"That's great!" Paula exclaimed excitedly. "Let's make that money, honey!" She raised her right hand in the air and Joe met her with his for a high five.

They continued to eat their ice cream in silence, but smiled at each other while playing footsie under the table and erotically feeding each other spoonfuls of ice cream. Just as they each reached across the table to give each other a cold kiss, Paula's personal phone vibrated. It was a text message. She thought about ignoring it, but she wondered who it could be. Angie and Michelle knew where she was and nobody else texted too often, other than Joe. So when she pressed the home button and Sean's name appeared, she was shocked. Then when she opened up the message and read the text – *Oh, so you into white dudes now?* – she was absolutely appalled. Her eyes widened and began to move vigorously in her head as she looked around the ice cream parlor in search of her ex. Joe could tell she was feeling disturbed from whatever she'd read.

"Everything okay?" he questioned.

"Sean just texted me. He saw us, or he can see us. I don't really know."

"Damn. He's not stalking you, is he?"

"I don't think so. This is the first I've heard from him since our lease ended."

"Okay, good. Well are you upset that he saw us together?" Joe continued to question Paula.

"No, not really. It's not that. It's just really complicated. Ten years is a long time to get over someone."

"I know. But I'm here now. I'll take care of you," Joe said to Paula, making her feel at ease.

She responded with a smile. She ignored the text from Sean for now, but knew she would definitely have to address it eventually.

"Did you see that shit? She was with a white dude!" Sean yelled at Damien as he drove them to their first delivery of the day.

"I saw it. You got something against white dudes?" Damien squinted his eyes at Sean.

"Naw, it's not like that but…"

"But what? My mom dated black men before she married my dad. You might've let Paula fall into the arms of her future husband!" Damien laughed.

"Man, kiss my ass," Sean replied angrily.

What if Paula *had* fallen in love? What if the white guy really *was* Paula's future husband? Even though Sean was still seeing Toni, he couldn't shake the thoughts and feelings he still had for Paula. And seeing her with another man, white or not, gave him a strong feeling of jealousy.

"What did you really expect, that she'd lock herself away in the top room of a castle and wait around for your ass to slay the dragon and come rescue her? And you got Toni anyway, so what's the problem? Oh yeah, I forgot. You still love Paula," Damien said shaking his head.

"It's just weird seeing her with somebody else. I know she's not gonna wait around, especially after how things ended, but I just never expected to see her with someone else. Damn!" Sean was getting frustrated with Damien again, but luckily they were just arriving at the location of Bridgette's house.

Charles had contacted Don't Shoot the Messenger to get rid of Bridgette. He explained that Bridgette was a very beautiful and successful woman, but she was all about money. Money drove every decision she made, even in their relationship. He'd met someone else who he connected with on a deeper and more spiritual level. It was time to let Bridgette know, but he didn't want to do it himself because he knew she'd try to coax him with money, so he called upon Sean and Damien to do his dirty work.

Sean pulled up to the astounding two story Victorian home. The evenly cut grass, trimmed hedges, and brick driveway had Sean and Damien's eyes glued. This was the kind of house they dreamed of owning one day in their future.

"Go do your thing," Sean encouraged Damien as he prepared to capture the images.

Damien stepped out of the van and proceeded past the brick driveway and walkway that led directly to the front door. He cautiously rang the doorbell and waited patiently for an answer. He turned on his recorder about one minute later as he saw the silhouette of a woman approaching.

"Who is it?" she asked loudly without opening the door.

"Hi. My name is Damien, and I'm with a company called Don't Shoot the Messenger. I was sent by a Mister Charles Michael. Do you know him?"

"Yes. What do you want with me? I've never heard of this business. There's no soliciting in this neighborhood. I don't know why Charles sent you here," she continued to talk through the door.

It was true; there was a sign that read NO SOLICITING when they entered the neighborhood. If only she'd had even the slightest clue as to what was about to transpire.

"Well ma'am, I am here to tell you that Charles does not want to see you anymore, and he would like to end the relationship."

All of a sudden, Damien heard the door unlock and then fly open.

"What did you just say?"

Charles wasn't lying when he said she was beautiful: caramel skin, brown eyes, long black hair, manicured nails, coke bottle shape with big breasts, *and* she had money! *What the hell was wrong with him?* Damien thought to himself.

"I'm sorry to inform you, but Charles does not want to continue a relationship with you." This was one of the hardest deliveries Damien ever had to do. Bridgette was fine as hell!

"Are you kidding me? Look at me!" Damien was already doing that. "I'm sexy. I have a good career. I have an extravagant home and drive a nice car. And I have money! What is there not to love?!"

Damien wondered the same exact thing. *I'll love you*, he thought to himself one more.

"Ma'am, I'm really sorry. I'm just delivering the message," Damien reluctantly answered.

Then Bridgette did something that was totally unexpected. She burst into tears. Damien turned to look at Sean who was all eyes, then he turned back to the damsel in distress.

"He said he loved me. We were supposed to get married. I already h-had my dress p-picked out." She mumbled through snot and tears.

Damien wanted to carry her upstairs and give her all the love she could ever want. Even her cry was sexy.

"Ma'am, you are a very beautiful woman. You will find love. Unfortunately, Charles is just not that guy," Damien said as gently as possible.

"How much does he want? Tell him to name his price, just please don't leave."

"Ma'am, he says that this isn't about money. I'm sorry."

Damien hated to have to end the conversation with Bridgette, but he had to. He and Sean had three more deliveries scheduled, and time was of the essence. He parted ways with Bridgette and wished her the best of luck before heading back to the van. She was still in tears as he walked away.

"Make sure you keep her address on file. I might have to come back and deliver some extra services if you know what I mean," Damien laughed and Sean joined him.

When he picked up his phone to get the address for the next delivery, Sean saw that he had one new text message. Paula finally responded with a short and straight forward text: *That's none of your damn business*. It was almost like getting stung by multiple bees simultaneously. It hurt. But Sean held it together. The last thing he wanted to hear was Damien's mouth. He closed the text message and looked up the next address. They were off to the next delivery.

It was a quiet day at the office. Tim wasn't expecting any clients and had no scheduled meetings. The only thing on his desk to do was a pile of paperwork and hopefully Christine if he got lucky. He buzzed through the intercom to the receptionist's desk.

"Christine, may I see you for a minute?"

"I'll be there shortly, Mr. Johnson," Christine replied.

Moments later, she appeared in Tim's office, shutting and locking the door behind her.

"I texted you last night," Tim said to her, standing up.

"I couldn't find my phone. I think little Nicky took it and hid it somewhere safe where Mommy can't find it. So what did the text say?"

"It didn't *say* anything," Tim said as he unzipped his pants, allowing his erect penis to breathe fresh air.

"Oh, I see," Christine smiled, grabbing and stroking it with her right hand.

But before they could fully dive into their sexual escapade, they could hear the bell ringing repeatedly at the receptionist's desk.

"Timothy fucking Johnson!"

Christine's eyes grew wider and her mouth dropped open.

"Oh, no! It's Doug!" Christine exclaimed looking at Tim, who was beginning to put his now limp dick back in his pants.

Doug was Christine's husband, a construction worker whose favorite pastime was boxing. They could hear him storming down the hall, busting open every door and the shouts of Tim's bewildered coworkers. When he got to Tim's locked office door, he shouted inside.

"Christine, you better not be in there!" He thrust his body into the door. It budged, but didn't break. It only took one more full body thrust to get through the locked door.

"Honey, please. You're embarrassing me! Why are you making a scene?" Christine asked her angry husband.

Doug pointed to Christine with his right index finger. "Don't say another fucking word." Then he turned to Tim and held up Christine's cell phone with the text Tim had sent the previous night. "Is this your dick on my wife's phone?"

Christine looked at the image with horror. Tim was silent for a moment, but he knew he had to say something. "It's not what you think," Tim tried to offer some silly excuse but Doug wasn't going for it.

Doug launched the phone in Tim's direction and quickly hopped over the desk that Tim had pleasured Doug's wife on so many times before. He threw a right punch that landed square on Tim's left cheekbone.

"Doug! Please, don't!" Christine begged her husband, but it was too late.

Tim tried to fight back as best he could, but it was pointless. He could not defend himself against Doug's punches, jabs, upper-cuts and blows to the body. All there was left for Tim to do was to put his arms up and shield his face. Luckily, a coworker called the police who soon arrived to save Tim from his brutal ass whooping. Doug was carried away in silver bracelets with Christine following not far behind. Tim, on the other hand, was carried away in an ambulance.

Luckily for Tim, upon his arrival to the hospital, he didn't need more than just a few bandages. Nothing was broken, however, he did suffer a concussion from the ordeal. The doctors kept him for a couple hours to monitor his condition before releasing him to the care of David. The last person he wanted the doctors to call was his wife.

"Dad! What happened?!" David was clearly shaken up by his dad's appearance.

"I'm okay, son. It was just an angry client. You know how some people can be about money," Tim lied to David with a bandaged straight face. But that was his story, and he was sticking to it.

Chapter Fifteen

The demand for Don't Shoot the Messenger services were still on the rise. Sean and Damien gloated on the way to their last delivery of the evening.

"I hoped that this business would be successful, but I didn't know people would be after us like this!" Damien exclaimed.

"What if we can expand and eventually be available nationwide?"

"That'd be crazy. We'd be making boss moves then and having other people do all the hard work for us. All we'd have to do is sit back and count our money. Residual income." Damien smiled and imagined counting stacks of Benjamins as he put both hands behind his head and leaned back against the headrest of the passenger seat.

"We'd be living the dream then," Sean added.

"Hell yeah, we would."

The GPS interrupted their daydreaming and signaled for Sean to make a left turn into the next neighborhood. He followed its directions and stopped in front of an old brick house. Damien wasted no time getting out of the van. The sun would be setting soon, and they didn't do deliveries in the dark.

Damien rang the doorbell but didn't hear it chime, so he knocked instead. Three firm knocks was enough to get Craig's attention. He opened the door.

"What's up? I ain't buying no candy."

Damien laughed. "Good, cause I'm not selling any."

"Well what do you want then?" Craig stood at the door with just a pair of North Carolina blue basketball shorts on and a pair of white socks. No shirt. The smell of marijuana was escaping and so too was the sound of West Coast rap music. Damien got the feeling that he was interrupting something.

"My name is Damien and I'm with a company called Don't Shoot the Messenger."

"And?" Craig asked, but not really seeking an answer.

"Loretta wanted us to let you know that she doesn't want to see you anymore. She asks that you never call her again because she knows that you're cheating on her."

Craig laughed hysterically. "Is that so?" He turned his head in the house and whistled. Damien hoped he wasn't calling for back-up. He didn't feel like fighting again.

To Damien's surprise, two females, both scantily dressed in their bras and panties, appeared on each side of Craig. One had the blunt in her hand before taking a puff and passing it to Craig.

"Make sure you tell Loretta she ain't the only one in town with a fat ass." That must've been the que for the other chick to turn around and make her ass cheeks clap while Craig gently tapped them.

Damien was momentarily mesmerized by the jiggling, but soon snapped out of it.

"Now if you'll excuse me," Craig continued, "I got some business to handle." The ladies giggled as he closed the door.

That was a Don't Shoot the Messenger first. Damien went back to the van.

"Well, Loretta was right. He's definitely cheating," Damien said to Sean before they both shared a hearty laugh. They were happy to end the business day on a funny note.

Sean dropped Damien off at his apartment before heading over to Toni's to spend the night with her.

Too tired to cook anything to eat or go out to buy fast food, Damien settled for a cold bowl of Frosted Flakes before taking a hot, steaming shower. He lay in bed in dark silence thinking about the possibilities of his and Sean's business. He was slowly drifting into sleep when his phone rang. He didn't recognize the number, but half sleep, answered anyway.

"Hello?"

"Hey, Damien," the voice on the other end said.

"Hey. Who's this?" Damien inquired with scrunched eyebrows.

"Oh, you don't recognize my voice?" she asked.

"Quit playing. Who is this?"

"Well, you left your card at my front door. You told me to call you. I followed your advice and finally let Aaron go for good."

"Kim?" Damien remembered and smiled. "It's nice to hear from you."

"Am I calling at a bad time?" Kim asked.

"No, not at all," Damien reassured, pretending to be wide awake. "So you say you finally got rid of Aaron?"

"I did. He was no good for me. It took me a long time to figure that out and you helped me with that. But everybody needs love, right?"

"Yeah, but not that kind of love," Damien said.

"What do you know about love? Have you ever been in love?" Kim asked.

"No. I can't say I have," Damien admitted.

"Surprise. Surprise."

Damien laughed. "What's that supposed to mean?"

"Nothing," Kim said. "I was really calling because I wanted to set some things straight. I think you got the wrong impression of me."

"Oh, really?"

"Yes, really. First of all, I live with my grandmother because I'm in school and I don't want to take out any student loans. I pay for my expenses out of pocket. Second of all, I don't have any kids, but I do have a niece and nephew whom are near and dear to my heart. Third of all, I was having a bad hair day *and* you came to my house to tell me I was being dumped. What kind of attitude did you expect me to have?"

"Wow." Silence. "Well, thank you for setting me straight. And I apologize for any assumptions I made about you." Damien definitely felt like an ass because all of the things that he had assumed about Kim turned out to be false. He was glad that she called to set the record straight. There was something about her that had him intrigued.

"Apology accepted," Kim replied.

The conversation between Kim and Damien lasted for about an hour before Damien could no longer fight off his sleep. But rather than thoughts of Don't Shoot the Messenger, he fell asleep with Kim now fresh on his mind.

After a thirty minute round of fast paced, sweaty sex, Toni snuggled her rear-end up close to Sean's crotch and they spooned in silence until Toni's words broke it.

"Sean, I really like you."

"I like you too, Toni."

Sean could sense that the dreaded conversation he'd been avoiding was about to happen with or without his consent.

"So, do you see this relationship going anywhere?"

There were a few seconds of silence which made Toni feel uneasy.

"I'm not sure. Just trying to take things slow and one day at a time," Sean replied.

"I understand that. But we've been taking it one day at a time for a few months now."

The silence was deafening.

Toni continued, "When's the last time you spoke to her?"

Confusion was plastered on Sean's face, but he obliged and answered her question, plus some.

"We don't really speak. But I saw her today."

"Saw her where?"

"Out with someone else."

"Did she see you?"

"No."

"So, how did you feel when you saw her?" Toni asked.

Sean thought for a minute before he responded. He knew that Toni probably wouldn't like his next answer, but complete honesty was his new policy.

"Well, I texted her to let her know that I saw her with someone else."

Toni rolled her body over to face Sean. Their faces were so close that they could feel the warmth from each other's breath.

"That sounds something like a jealous text to me," Toni said.

"Call it what you want. It could be that," Sean said frankly.

"So, let me get this straight. You saw your ex today with another man and you sent her what sounds like a jealous text. Now you're here in my bed and you can't even tell me where you see this going?"

"Well, yes, but I think you're taking it the wrong way."

"And what way is that?" Toni questioned.

Sean turned to lay flat on his back. He stared at the ceiling in frustration. "It's just complicated."

"Well, let me help make it a little less complicated. I think you should go home."

"Why?" Sean boldly asked.

Toni stared at him for a moment before saying anything. She tried to keep her composure while she spoke. "Sean, you are clearly confused and the last thing I need is confusion in my life. I asked you were you sure you wanted to date exclusively a while ago and you assured me that you were. Right now, you sound like a confused little boy and you need to roll your ass out of my bed and go lay your head on your own pillow tonight."

Toni stood up and waited for Sean to get his belongings together. She led the way to the front door and said nothing as Sean crossed the doorway. She closed the door behind him and rolled her eyes before heading back to her room to get some much deserved shuteye.

Chapter Sixteen

Sean had a restless night after Toni put him out. He understood her frustration but still felt as if she had overreacted. He decided to transfer his energy into the business. There was never a wrong time to check messages, emails, and voicemails from potential clients.

Sean always began with voicemails. There were never as many voicemails as there were Facebook messages and emails. The interaction between people in society over the years had taken a strong turn towards more electronic communication than face-to-face or verbal communication. Maybe that was one reason why people needed his and Damien's services. But what did that say about him? He needed that same service before it even became one. Nevertheless, he took notes as he listened to the four voices. Then he moved on to the nine Facebook messages and seven emails. The messages were all pretty generic, but there was nothing on the face of the planet Earth that could have prepared Sean for the very last email he read.

He reached for his phone in a panic to call his best friend and business partner. The phone rang four times with Sean growing in anticipation after each ring.

"It's five in the morning," Damien said in a harsh tone without even saying, "Hello."

Sean didn't care; he couldn't care about the time. "I know what time it is, but you need to come over here right now."

"I have a workout session at six. I can't."

"No. You don't understand the severity of the situation. I need for you get up and get over here ASAP!"

"I don't have time for this fuckery. If this is about Paula—''

Sean didn't let him finish. "Shut up and get your ass over here now!" Sean needed Damien to realize just how serious the situation was without spelling it out over the phone. That last email was something that Damien would have to read on his own.

Thirty minutes passed before Damien's fist finally came to blows with Sean's door. He ran to open it.

"What the hell is going on? It better be good."

Sean didn't say a word. He didn't have to. The words on the computer screen would speak volumes for themselves. He pointed to the dimly lit screen and Damien followed his cue. Damien walked over to the couch and read the email. He read silently, but the silent words filled the room with a piercing noise, such a noise that would leave ringing in his ears afterwards.

Don't Shoot the Messenger,

My name is Joseph Hall and I am requesting your services to break up with my girlfriend of six months. Her name is Deborah Johnson, and she is a married woman. I thought we were falling in love and that she'd leave her husband like she promised she would, but she has not been a woman of her word. She claimed that her marriage had been on the rocks and that her husband had been seeing someone else. I believed her, and I can't understand why she won't just leave him. I refuse to continue to aid in her adulterous actions, yet she continues to contact me. I want out, as I have expressed to her. I hope that your business will be able to assist me with this matter. Thank you in advance.

Joseph Hall

Damien's entire body was filled with rage and everything in the room was the same color, even Sean – deep crimson like fresh blood. He rushed around the red couch, grabbed Sean by his red neck and squeezed, forcing him against the red door.

"Is this a fucking joke? You know this dude?" Damien questioned in extreme anger.

Coughing and hitting at Damien's arm, Sean screamed, "No! This isn't a joke! I wouldn't joke about no shit like this! Let. Me. Go!"

Sean was starting to struggle through the red and Damien could see that. He was also convinced that this was no hoax and he needed to get to the bottom of it.

"Call him!"

"What?" Sean questioned, still trying to catch his breath.

"Call him! Our clients have to have proof that they're in a relationship, right? I wanna see the proof, and whoever the hell this Joseph Hall dude is."

As Damien asked, Sean called Joe, and they agreed to meet two hours later at a public park. It was the longest one hundred and twenty minutes of Damien's life. He had done so many sit-ups and push-ups that he'd lost count, but there was no pain or soreness. The adrenaline rushing through his body made him feel like The Hulk and he literally wanted to smash everything in sight.

When they got in the van to go to meet their potential client, Sean tried his best to calm Damien down and assure him that he would find out what was going on. Nothing worked, and why would it? He just found out that his mom was cheating on his dad and was about to go meet her manstress. He was beyond pissed.

When they arrived at the park, they agreed that Damien would remain in the van. There was just no telling what he was capable of doing at that moment. Plus, that was a part of Sean's normal duty anyway.

At the entrance of the park was a beautiful water fountain filled with clear blue water and water spewing from eight sprouts all around it. The bottom was laced with pennies and just slightly drizzled with silver coins. That was the meeting spot.

Joe was already there, seated on the gray brick of the water fountain in jeans, a t-shirt, and baseball cap. Sean approached him, paperwork in hand.

"Joe?" Sean asked.

"Yes," Joe answered, standing up.

"Nice to meet you. I'm Sean with Don't Shoot the Messenger." They firmly shook hands. "Let's get straight to business, shall we?"

"Sure," Joe agreed, sitting back down.

"Before we do business with any client, we first have to confirm that a relationship actually exists for between the two parties."

"Understood," Joe nodded his head as he spoke. He then began to make his phone come alive with his right thumb. Joe admitted to not having a substantial amount of hard evidence, as his and Deborah's relationship was a secret, but what he did have – a couple photos and a few text messages – was pretty damaging.

"And how long have you been dating Deborah?"

"It's been about six months," Joe answered.

"Where did you guys me—"

Damien's shrieking voice drowned out the rest of Sean's question.

"Did you fuck her motherfucker?!" Damien yanked Joe by the collar and yelled in his face. "Answer the question!"

Joe was struggling to grasp not only air but also what was happening. He took a hard look at the young man who currently had him hemmed up.

"Damien?" Joe asked.

Damien's grip loosened a bit. Not because he was any less angry, but simply because he didn't understand how this guy knew his name.

"Who are you?" How do you know my name?" Damien questioned the mysterious man.

Joe's eyes widened with shock. He escaped from the grip Damien had on him and ran in the opposite direction. Damien's instinct told him to chase Joe, but Sean grabbed his shoulder before he could take his first stride.

"No. Don't. We're gonna get to the bottom of this," Sean said reassuringly.

Sean led the unwilling Damien back to the van.

"Take me to my parents' house," Damien said sternly.

About thirty minutes later, they pulled into the driveway of the beautiful Johnson home. The van didn't even come to a complete stop before Damien hopped out of the moving vehicle and rushed to the front door with Sean on his heels. He reached down into the pit of his right pocket and pulled out some lent and his keys. Once the door was opened, time seemed to lose track of itself.

"Mom!" Damien stormed through the foyer hollering, "Mom!"

David and Tim were both prompted out of their rooms at the sound of Damien's screaming voice.

"Damien, why are you yelling?" Tim asked angrily with his eyebrows stretched.

"Where's Mom?" Damien continued to ask. "Is she in the room?"

"I don't know where she is," Tim answered.

"She had to run a couple of errands," David said, entering the living room.

"You still didn't answer my question," Tim stated.

Damien's piercing eyes remained locked on Tim's face.

"I can't answer that right now. But I will ask you this question one more time: Are you cheating on Mom?"

"My answer to that will never change and you, Damien, will NOT question me again!" Tim pointed his right index finger towards Damien.

Father and eldest son gazed angrily at each other. The only thing that altered the staring was the sound of the garage opening. Deborah was home. Damien stormed out the door before the garage could even finish going up. Deborah saw him and smiled while slowly easing the car inside. She put the gear in park and got out.

"Hey son. You going to help me with my bags?" Deb smiled at Damien.

"Who the hell is Joe?" Damien demanded.

The smile Deborah was wearing quickly faded.

"Who the hell are you talking to, boy?" Deborah changed her tone to let Damien know just who was in charge. But Damien didn't seem to be phased.

"Who is Joe?" He questioned his mother again.

"Who wants to know?" Deb retorted.

"Me, Mom, me! Who is Joe and why is he calling my business trying to break up with you?"

"What?" Deb's face was smothered in disarray.

Deborah snatched the bags out of her car and stormed past Damien into the house. Damien followed right behind her.

"All this time you've been accusing Dad of cheating when it was really you all along."

"Wait. What?" David wasn't sure he'd heard his brother correctly.

"Go ahead, Mom. Tell them who Joe is."

"Joe is just my coworker. Damien what the hell is going on?" Deborah was becoming quite agitated with Damien's allegations.

"You tell us what's going on. Why did Joe email Don't Shoot the Messenger asking us to break up with you for him? He showed Sean pictures and text messages."

Everybody momentarily glanced at Sean, who tried to shrink himself even further into the couch, but it was pointless.

"Deborah, is this true?" Tim asked. "Are you seeing someone else?"

"Tim, don't you dare question me about cheating," Deborah angrily gritted the words through her teeth.

"Deb, they seem to have proof of your infidelity." Tim put his head down before the next words slithered out of his mouth. "After all of the shit you put me through, I think you should be the one to leave."

Deborah was stunned. She searched for reassurance from her boys, but received nothing except for stares in agreement with their father.

"You boys have finally let your father's manipulation get the best of you. After all the shit I do for you, this is how you repay me, your own mother! I know my baby boy, Donovan, would defend his mother if he were here."

No one spoke. She slowly walked toward Tim and stood directly in front of him, staring at him through dark and rage filled eyes that spoke words of hate. After her eyes spoke, her right hand took a turn, slapping Tim with a mighty force that made slob linger from his bottom lip. His only reaction was to grab his left cheek, as if trying to hold the sting from releasing, but he could feel it full force.

Deborah grabbed her belongings and walked gracefully back into the garage to get in her car and leave. She wasn't leaving because they wanted her to. She was leaving because she was going to find out just what the hell Joe was really up to.

Chapter Seventeen

After the previous day's events, Damien didn't feel up to the next few deliveries, so he sought out the help of his brothers, David and Donovan. Sean was not pleased with Damien's decision to skip out on the day's deliveries, but understood and respected it. He was, however, happy to be gaining two sets of hands, especially since the next delivery involved heavy lifting.

Tracy needed the assistance of Don't Shoot the Messenger to break up with her boyfriend of three years. She described Marion as a very fidgety man who was prone to emotional outbursts. He'd lost several jobs as a result. Tracy had attempted to leave before, but Marion had somehow tracked her down and dragged her home by the roots of her hair. She was sure that this time he'd never find her, but she had to execute the plan to make a clean escape.

When Sean, David and Donovan arrived to the two story townhouse that Tracy and Marion shared, they began transporting items from inside out to the van very quickly. David and Donovan started upstairs while Sean spoke to Tracy downstairs.

"How are you, Tracy? Ready for the big move?" Sean questioned. He could see that something was bothering her.

"I'm nervous. We have to hurry. I couldn't sleep at all last night. He knows something is up. He must." Tracy bit her nails as she spoke and her right leg bounced up and down vigorously.

"Everything will be fine. We'll get you out of here safe and sound."

The reassurance of Sean's words didn't last long. A few minutes passed before Tracy's panic was full blown.

"We have to go now. I don't care what's left. I just have to get out of here." Tracy was shaking uncontrollably, and Sean attempted to console her. Sean soon released his grip so he could run upstairs to get Tracy's purse. She was so distraught she could hardly move. The twins ran back inside to get a cold cup of water before they were to depart.

The devil was at work that day because in the short amount of time Sean ran upstairs to get Tracy's purse and the twins went to the kitchen to quench their thirst, Marion pulled up in the driveway and parked right next to the van. He pulled his gun out of the glove box and got out. He lifted up his shirt in the back and placed the gun inside his pants, letting the shirt fall back down over it. He slammed the car door and swiftly strolled to the front door.

Tracy heard the sound of a door close and panic rushed over her body like an uncontrollable flood. She stood up, but her feet were like cement stuck to the floor. Before she could shout Sean's name, the front door opened and Marion's brown eyes were digging into her skin.

"What the hell is going on up in here?"

Tracy was frozen in time. The only thing that moved on her body were her eyes as they'd grown wider with shock. She couldn't even tell if her heart still beat; she felt like she was short of breath and losing air every time she inhaled. But yet, she stood.

The sound of Marion's voice prompted David and Donovan out of the kitchen and into the living room. The sight of them, in turn, prompted Marion to draw his gun. The twins' hands flew to the roof.

"Whoa! No need for that," David tried to negotiate.

"Who the fuck are y'all?"

The footsteps coming down the stairs interfered with the answer to Marion's question. The gun shifted directions from the twins to Sean. Sean, with purse in hand, stopped before he could reach the bottom.

"Who is this nigga with your purse in his hand coming down my stairs like he lives here?" Marion asked yet another question, directing his attention to Tracy, but still aiming the gun at Sean.

"Umm…" Tracy stammered trying to locate the right words in her mind.

"Hey, Marion. We're just a few of Tracy's cousins visiting from out of town." Sean jumped in to save Tracy from drowning.

"Cousins," Marion said with a smirk. "Didn't I tell you the next time you tried to leave me, I'd kill your ass?"

"Oh, it's nothing like that. We're just going out to the mall and to grab a bite to eat," Sean stated, giving Tracy a look for her to chime in any second now.

"Babe, it's nothing. Really. I was gonna call you and ask you if you wanted me to bring you anything back. They were just driving through and stopped by," Tracy tried to keep her trembling voice from cracking.

Sean slowly began to walk down the remaining three stairs, but immediately stopped when Marion's right thumb pulled back to release the safety on the gun.

"Y'all must be trying to play me for a fool. I might be crazy, but I ain't never been nobody's fool. I told this bitch I would kill her, and I'm a man of my word."

The tears started to well up in Tracy's eyes. She never imagined as a little girl that her life would end up this way, loving an abusive and controlling man, the same type of man her mother escaped from. Pregnant with Tracy at seventeen, Tracy's mother ran away from an abusive forty-two year old man. Tracy had suffered two miscarriages as a result of Marion's abuse. But she was never saddened by the loss of her children because she wasn't prepared to withstand the guilt she knew she'd carry within her if she brought an innocent life into the world with Marion as the father. Tracy's mother at least was able to get away from her haunted relationship, but at whose expense because there Tracy stood with her life hanging in the balance.

"Just kill me, already. Set me free," Tracy stared Marion in his devilish eyes.

"Tracy, no!" Sean shouted.

Marion pointed the gun once again at Tracy, allowing the barrel to stare her in the eye. It saw such beauty in her, beauty that its bullets could ruin. Marion decided to answer her prayers at that moment and pulled the trigger. The bullet penetrated her chest and forced her body to the floor. The blood began to spread like an overflowing tub of water. Sean took off running to assist Tracy, but Marion pulled the trigger again.

The twins charged at Marion like two defensive ends trying to tackle the quarterback on third down with inches to go. Donovan punched while David wrestled the gun out of Marion's hand. Sweat trickled from his forehead as he tried to avoid grabbing the trigger. Once he had it, Donovan ran to Sean's side, pulling out his cell phone to dial 911. Donovan tried his best to keep both Tracy and Sean calm until the ambulance arrived, but Tracy was a little too calm. He knelt down to check on her once more, but her chest no longer moved up and down. He placed his finger directly beneath her nose, but warm air no longer escaped her body. He grabbed her wrist, then checked her neck, but he could feel no pulse.

"David, I think she's dead."

"What? Check again! Are you sure?" David questioned his brother.

"Told that bitch I'd kill her," Marion grinned.

"Shut up before I kill your dumb ass," David retorted, pointing the gun at Marion.

Donovan returned to Sean's side and put his hand over Sean's hand that covered the hole in his abdomen.

"I'm sorry," Sean whispered to Donovan.

"You don't have anything to be sorry about. Don't talk. Save your energy. Like Ike said, 'If you die, I'll kill ya.'" Donovan let out a light chuckle and Sean smiled.

The faint sound of sirens drew nearer and nearer, and the twins gave each other a glance of relief.

Deb spent the whole drive cursing Tim out loud in her car, but when she arrived to her workplace, all of her focus shifted to Joe. She spotted his white Infiniti in the parking lot and knew she had to think fast.

She discretely made her way to her second floor corner office with only one person seeing her. She opened her bottom desk drawer and removed the lighter she used to light the Febreeze candle resting on her desk. She rolled her chair over directly beneath the smoke detector and lifted herself up, being careful to keep her balance and not to make the wheels on the chair roll.

With her right thumb, she made the flame come alive and slowly began to wave the heat beneath the detector. With some patience, after about two minutes, the fire alarm was set off. Deborah hopped out of the chair and hid beneath her desk as everyone else in the office exited the building.

When the coast was clear, Deborah raced to Joe's office determined to find some intimidating evidence. Luckily, because of the sudden fire alarm, Joe left his computer without logging out. Deborah quickly made his work email appear on the screen. She scrolled and skimmed from page to page, but found nothing.

Giving up on the email, Deborah searched around Joe's desk to see if she'd luck up there. Nothing on top of his desk stood out, but when she pulled opened the drawer, the first thing she noticed was Tim's business card. She flipped it over on the back and found Tim's personal cell number and Google email address.

Feeling like her luck was improving, she pulled up Google mail on Joe's computer, and to her satisfaction, the computer's memory already had the password entered. All she had to do was click "log in" to gain total access.

Seeing the name Timothy Johnson made her left click right away, and she found herself viewing an incriminating thread of messages between the two men. She hastily printed the email without any second thoughts.

Having the attorney mindset she had, Deborah didn't stop there. She soon discovered the email that was sent to Don't Shoot the Messenger. The pieces of the puzzle were all beginning to form a bigger picture. Tim was providing Joe with free financial services as long as he set Deborah up to make it look like she was the adulterer in the relationship.

Deborah, although feeling quite disturbed, was relieved to know the truth behind the madness that was her husband.

When the fire alarm finally stopped, Deborah knew she had to make a quick exit before her coworkers began to file back inside. Just as she was about to move the mouse to the red X in the top right corner, she saw the name Paula Davis. The muffled voices were becoming clearer with each passing second and Deborah knew she had to act quickly. She opened the email, pressed the print button and closed out the window on the screen. She grabbed the papers out of Joe's desk printer before sneaking back to the safety of her office.

Damien had left his parents' house feeling extremely distraught about what had happened with his mom. He needed an outlet, someone to talk to and confide in. He picked up his phone and sent a short text to Kim to get her attention.

Her response was immediate which made a smile flash across Damien's face.

Damien, staying true to who he was, still found time after deliveries to fit in one-night stands here and there. He could get as much sex as he desired, but what he lacked was someone he could have a real conversation with. All of the heartbreaks that he and Sean had been delivering seemed to be having an effect on him.

Thinking about what he was going to text Kim next and beginning to enter the words, he was interrupted by David's face in the middle of his screen.

"What up?" Damien answered.

Filled with panic, David yelled into the receiver, "You gotta come to the hospital!"

Damien could hear the sirens in the background.

"What the hell happened?"

"Just come! It's Sean. He's hurt bad. Get here quick!"

David's choppy response and panicky voice made Damien hop up and race to his car. He left in a rush in the direction of the hospital.

Chapter Eighteen

Several family and friends, including Sean's parents, Cassie and Harold, other relatives, Paula and her parents, the twins, Damien, Tim, and Deborah, gathered at the hospital to check on the status of Sean. He was in the middle of surgery, so everyone congregated in a freezing cold waiting area.

Deborah opened her arms to embrace Cassie and she fell into Deb's arms in full blown tears.

"That's my baby in there," Cassie's words stammered through her cries.

"I know, sweetie. He's going to be just fine. You hear me? We just need to keep the prayers going," Deborah said. The silent whimpers continued for hours as Sean underwent emergency surgery. Upon its completion, the doctor expressed to the family that he was in recovery and would not be able to accept any visitors. Disappointed, but high in spirits, everyone agreed to return the following morning.

Once exiting the hospital's sliding glass doors, everyone began to disperse in their separate ways.

Deborah had purposely parked her car adjacent to Damien's in attempt to have a quick word with him upon leaving the hospital and the plan had panned out.

"Damien!" she called to get his attention.

He turned and slowly headed to the driver's side of her car where she stood.

About one foot of space separated the two as they stood face to face. After about thirty seconds of silence, Deborah grabbed her son's face between her thumb and four fingers.

"Don't you ever disrespect me like you did the other day, and in my house! I brought you in this world; I can and I will take you out! You understand me?"

"Yes, Ma!" Damien struggled to get his face out of her grip.

"Now that that's out of the way, I have something I need to show you. I'm staying at the Ramada Inn. Follow me," Deb said.

"Okay," Damien agreed with no hesitation.

Damien followed his mother's every turn until they arrived at the hotel. Then he followed her footsteps inside.

"Mrs. Johnson, you're back. And with a guest, I see," the attendant behind the desk said.

"Pedro, this is my oldest son, Damien. Thank you for being so observant, though," Deborah replied with a sarcastic smile.

Pedro gave Damien a wave and Damien half waved back.

They took the elevator to the fourth floor and Damien trailed his mom down the narrow, dimly lit hall until they reached room 426. She slid her key down into the slot and when the green light lit up, she pushed the door open. It slammed shut and locked automatically behind Damien.

Tim and Joe's paper trail of lies lay meticulously across Deborah's hotel queen sized bed. She handed the papers to Damien in a strategic order, showing first how Tim and Joe were attempting to drown her in a pool of tales from the dark side and ending with evidence of an obvious romance between Paula and Joe.

"How did you get this?"

"It doesn't matter. But you didn't think I was going to go down without a fight, did you?" Deborah said.

"Wait. So, Dad and Joe are in cahoots and Paula and Joe are dating?" Damien asked.

"It seems that way," Deborah confirmed.

"So does Paula know about Dad and Joe's lies?"

"Well, from the messages I've read, it doesn't seem so, but I can't be too sure," Damien's mom replied. "So, are you thinking what I'm thinking?"

"No, Mom. Me and my brothers will handle this," Damien said.

"So, you don't want me to do anything?" Deb asked, almost disappointed.

"No. I got it," Damien replied. He held onto the papers as he exited the hotel room.

When Damien got home that night, all he could think to do was call Kim and tell her everything that went on the past few days.

"I'm really sorry about your friend," Kim said.

"I just feel like it's my fault 'cause I wasn't there."

"But what would that have changed? Then you might've been shot, too. You can't blame yourself for someone else's actions," Kim said.

"You're probably right, but it still doesn't change the way I feel about the situation."

"So, what are you guys gonna do about your business?"

"I don't even know. To tell you the truth, who's to say something like this won't happen again? Building a business and a name for ourselves isn't worth getting shot over. I'm too damn pretty for a bullet," Damien said and smiled.

Kim chuckled in return and said, "Maybe after Sean recovers, you guys could change the basis of the company around. You know, rather than tearing people apart, you could bring them together."

"Maybe. I don't know. But I have a long day ahead of me tomorrow, so I'm gonna get some sleep," Damien said.

"Okay," Kim replied. "Good luck with your dad."

It was really Tim who was going to need the luck.

Chapter Nineteen

Between Sean getting shot, the truth he was discovering about his dad, and the feelings he was starting to develop for Kim, Damien couldn't sleep at all.

The Don't Shoot the Messenger Facebook page had gotten some messages over the past couple of days. Damien usually ignored them and just let Sean handle that part of the business, but because of the circumstances, he decided to read the messages himself.

Not intrigued by any of them, he decided to check their email. It was then that he realized why his dad tried to set his mom up. A break up email from Christine was the last piece of this unsolved mystery. Damien excelled in math in school, so he quickly put two and two together.

Tim wanted to divorce Deborah, but wanted to make it look like it was because of her infidelity. He enlisted the assistance of Joe after he gave Sean and Damien's business the green light. Tim intended to be with Christine, but judging by her email, her feelings were no longer mutual.

Dear Don't Shoot the Messenger,

I write this letter knowing the many sins I have committed will finally face the light, but I know that this is the right thing to do. I am a married woman and I love my husband dearly, but I have been carrying on an adulterous affair with a married man whom I work with. For the sake of my marriage, please help me to not only quit my job, but also to end this poisonous relationship with Tim Johnson. I have tried to break things off in the past, but he has made it extremely difficult and I have been too weak. Please contact me if your business can be of any assistance to me. I can best be reached at 407-555-9467.

Damien was floored. He never imagined in his most horrific nightmares that anything like this could ever transpire in his family. Damien had some important decisions to make, and soon.

He decided to get dressed and head to hospital to see Sean an hour before everyone else was supposed to arrive.

Paula opened her eyes to discover that Joe was already awake, staring at her in her sleep. It was flattering yet creepy at the same time.

"Good morning," Joe said with a smile.

"Good morning," Paula replied.

He kissed her cheek and pulled her close. "So what are we doing today?"

"Well, I'm going back to hospital in a little bit and later I have to go meet a client. I'm starting a new renovation today," Paula said.

Paula could see the look of disappointment on Joe's face. He wanted so badly to tell her the truth about his conspiracy with Tim, but the fear of not waking up to her beauty and warmth gave him reservations.

"Can I at least cook you breakfast?" he asked.

"Of course you can," Paula said. Breakfast was her favorite meal of the day. No way was she turning that down. "I'm going to shower."

She stood up and Joe followed, his erect morning penis snuggled up close to Paula's plump behind while his arms wrapped around her body and his hands caressed her stomach. Paula turned on the shower and turned around to face Joe. He lifted his shirt that she was wearing over her head, watching her nipples come to life, then pulled her panties down. Pulling like magnets, their lips came together. It was hard to tell whether the steam rising in the air was coming from the shower or their bodies.

He turned her around, entering her through the back door. She leaned slightly, placing her hands on the counter and moaning with pleasure. They gazed at their reflections of each other in the mirror. Joe bit his bottom lip as gratification filled every inch of his body. After several strokes, he picked her up, allowing her legs to straddle around his waist. He pinned her body against the wall, and her back moved up and down as he went in and out. Her left breast found its way into his mouth and he gently bit down on her nipple as he climaxed. A morning quickie at its finest.

They both inhaled and exhaled heavily before stepping into the shower. Joe washed quickly so he could cook Paula's breakfast. Paula stayed in a while longer, allowing the steaming hot water to run down her back as she had thoughts of Joe being the man of her dreams. There were so many things right about him, she couldn't imagine anything that could change her mind.

Damien pulled up a chair next to Sean's hospital bed. Seeing all the tubes in him and the machine helping him breathe made Damien feel uneasy. He spoke to Sean as if Sean were wide awake, alert, and could hear everything he was saying.

"Man, I hate seeing you like this," Damien said. He dropped his head in the palms of his hands for a few seconds before lifting it and speaking again. "Is this what our business has come to? People getting shot and families being torn apart? I didn't get in it for this. There's no amount of money in the world worth your life or the love of my family. I'm sorry about all the shit I gave you about Paula. What y'all had was real love and I feel like I played a part in ruining that. Truth is, I admire the love you had for her."

He took a pause, wiping away the tears that lightly drizzled down his face. He looked at Sean's face once more and said, "I can't do this Don't Shoot the Messenger shit without you. I'm sending a message to everyone telling them that all services will be canceled until you come back. They can figure their own shit own."

He stood up over Sean, looking down on him. He lowered his head onto Sean's chest and cried out, "It's not the same without you, man. Hurry up and wake yo' ass up!"

The tears that drizzled before were now becoming steadier. But when Sean's heart rate monitor flat lined, the tears heavily drained from Damien's eye lids. One nurse rushed in, then two, and three, urging Damien out of the way and completely out of the room. As he was being pushed out, the doctor rushed in and slammed the door behind him. Another nurse moved Damien to a waiting area where he and his tears were left to wonder about the status of his best friend.

Chapter Twenty

    While Sean was still in the hospital battling for his life, Damien had one final delivery he had to make with the help of his brothers.

    After they'd met up with Christine and saw the tons of evidence of her and Tim's relationship, they devised a plan to bring him down. Damien didn't like Christine for her involvement in the adultery, but he had to focus on the bigger picture, which was Tim. Not only was he having an affair, but he lied about it over and over again *and* tried to set his mom up. Damien had to put a stop to the madness.

    The three brothers pulled up to their dad's financial office in order to carry out the plan. When they walked in, that was Christine's cue. She buzzed Tim's office.

    "Mr. Johnson, you have a delivery. Would you like for me to bring it back?" Christine asked.

    "Yes, Christine. Please bring it back."

    Christine stood up from behind her receptionist area and the trio waited for her to strut her stuff into their dad's office. If she was in there for more than three minutes with the door closed, then they would be busting in on that party. She carried with her the package that had actually been delivered earlier that morning.

    She entered the office and closed the door behind her. With an outstretched right arm, she handed the package to Tim. He accepted it without even looking up. He was in the middle of what sounded like a heated conversation and he immediately shooed Christine away.

"Why didn't you tell me that was your son's business?" Joe asked angrily.

"You didn't ask," Tim replied.

"Fuck you."

"A deal is a deal and you're not done yet," Tim said.

"The deal's off. Go to hell." Joe hung up the phone.

Tim slammed his cell phone down on his desk and thought about his next move.

Damien, David, and Donovan were disappointed to see Christine ambling back to her desk so soon. They were going to have to wait a little longer. They wanted to keep their presence in the office discreet until it was time for the actual delivery, so they decided to head back out to the parking lot.

Quicker than Christine's butt was able to leave a print in her chair, Tim intercomed her to come back to his office. She agreed, then ran to the glass door to call the boys back.

"Psst!"

They all turned around in unison. She looked at them with wide eyes, then scurried back to Tim's office. The brothers rushed back in to prepare for action.

Christine could barely get back in Tim's office door all the way before he was kissing and fondling her. Christine was immediately filled with discomfort. She didn't know if it was because of Tim's current aggressiveness or because she knew she was ending the affair with him. Either way, she almost wanted to throw up in her mouth a little, but she knew she had to keep up the act. He lifted up her skirt and she pretended to enjoy it.

Just as he was unbuttoning his slacks to release the pressure that had built up, his three sons busted through the door with their cell phones out snapping pictures and capturing video of Tim cheating in the act.

"Oh, so you're not cheating on Mom? You're just so innocent, huh?" Donovan questioned his father.

"Then you tried to frame Mom and make her look like the one who was cheating when all along it was you," David added as Tim zipped his pants and tried to shield his face.

"And we have proof, so you can wipe that, 'What the fuck?' look off your face." Damien started throwing the emails in the air to show Tim how deep of a hole he had dug himself. "You left a paper trail. I thought you were smarter than that. I thought a lot of things about you, but I guess I was wrong. And we watched Mom throw all your shit out, so don't even think about showing your face at her house. Oh, and she quit, starting now," Damien said pointing to Christine. "She's done with you and staying with her husband, so find yourself another bitch."

They all stopped recording at the same. Christine didn't have time to be offended at being called a bitch. She pulled herself together before leading Damien and his brothers out of Tim's office. As they exited, they saw that they had drawn the attention of some of the other employees. Tim was left to explain to them, or at least try to explain, all of the ruckus in his office, again.

Paula was no fan of Damien, but when he reached out to her, she agreed to meet him for lunch. She figured the topic of conversation would probably be about Sean.

They met for lunch at Sea Food Frenzy. Despite not liking each other, they both loved sea food.

Damien was already there when Paula arrived. He stood up to greet her with a slight hug as she approached and sat down at the two seater table.

"How are you? I got you a glass of water until we order," Damien said.

"Thank you. I'm well, and yourself?" Paula asked.

"I could be better, but I'm alive, in one piece, and in good health, so I can't complain too much."

"Well, that's good. So, what's up? Why are we here?" Paula wasn't interested in wasting time with small talk and catching up. She wanted to get straight to the point.

"First and foremost, and I know you probably don't want to hear this, but I'm sorry about the way things ended between you and Sean. I know I played a big role and I want to apologize for that."

Paula stared blankly at Damien, sipping her water real slow.

"Do you accept my apology?" Damien questioned. If he was going to apologize, the least she could do was acknowledge it.

"Apology accepted. But that can't be the only reason you invited me here," Paula said.

The waiter returned to take their orders.

"My name is Brad, and I'll be serving you today. Can I start you guys off with some crab cakes?"

"No, thanks," the pair said at once.

"Ladies first," Damien said, being a gentleman.

Paula proceeded with her order. "I'll have the fried shrimp with fries and steamed broccoli," Paula said.

"And you, sir?"

"I'll have the seafood sampler," Damien said to the waiter.

Brad picked up their menus and said, "I'll have your orders out as soon as possible."

"Thank you," Paula said to the waiter.

"So, where were we?" Damien asked.

"Why did you really bring me here?"

"Well, I also wanted you to know that Sean is still in love with you," Damien said.

Paula could feel her cheeks turn rosy red. "As much as I still have a ton of love for Sean in my heart, this is what he wanted, so this is how it is. I hate to see him hurt though. It's breaking my heart," Paula sighed.

"I know you're dating someone else, and that's your business—"

"Don't," Paula cut him off. "Let's not get into this because I'm sure Sean is seeing someone else as well," Paula said.

"It's not about that," said Damien.

"Then what is it about?"

"The guy that you're seeing, Joe right?" Damien asked?

"Umm, how do you know his name? What in the hell is this?" Paula questioned Damien with shriveled eyebrows.

"Calm down."

"No! What could you possibly have to tell me about the man I'm dating whom you don't even know? I'm out!" Paula shoved her chair back with force and stood up angrily, grabbing her purse.

"Paula, please!" Damien grabbed her forearm, but her facial expression made him loosen his grip. "It's important and it's only in your best interest." Damien looked at her with pleading eyes.

Paula could see that he was serious, so she sat back down, after snatching her arm away.

"I will try to give you the abridged version, but still tell you the whole story. When your boyfriend first moved here, he got financial services from my dad and he happened to work at the same law firm as my mother as well. He got your business card from my dad's office and yeah…you guys happened, I guess. My parents' marriage has been on the rocks for some time, and I don't think my father was prepared to take the blame for its downfall. Therefore, he went to Joe for help to frame my mother. So, your boyfriend has been swindling his way close to my mom and reporting back to my dad. Then, prompted by my dad of course, Joe came to

Sean and me, well our business, not knowing it was *our* business, to "break up" with my mom. In the end, my brothers and I discovered that it was all a lie, and the real truth was that my dad was cheating on my mom the whole time." Damien took a sip of his water wishing that it were a mixture of Coke and Hennessey instead.

Paula was quite stunned by Damien's new revelations.

"You do with the information what you want, but I thought you should know what kind of scheme your man was involved in," Damien said.

"Thank you for sharing. I'm. Really. Speechless. I really don't know what to say," said Paula. She paused, and with hesitation said, "So just for clarification, to what extent did the "relationship" between Joe and your mom extend to?"

"I'm not really sure exactly. I know they didn't have sex or anything. Eww. Just thinking about my mom doing it makes me sick. But whatever happened between them, it was because Joe had ill intentions, so I suppose he tried to get her to do whatever he could for the purposes of upholding his end to whatever agreement he and my dad had."

"Waiter!" She yelled out when she spotted their waiter coming out of the kitchen area. "What was his name again?" She directed her question towards Damien, but then it hit her and she blurted out, "Brad! Brad!"

He sped over to the table.

"Can I please get a long island?" Paula asked.

"Sure," said Brad. "Do you have your ID?"

"Seriously?" Paula pulled out her driver's license. She wasn't upset that Brad ID'd her, she was just extremely aggravated at the news she'd just received.

"While you're here," Damien chimed in, "let me get a Hen and Coke."

"Sure. Your ID as well," said Brad smiling. He took their orders and walked to the next table to check on the family of four.

"So the story was so intense that you needed a drink?" Damien asked, smiling.

"Yes. And depending on how I feel after the first one, I might need a second one," Paula replied.

They both laughed lightly and were happy to see the food and drinks arrive at the same time. They ate and drank in peace, and even gave each other a friendly embrace as they left.

Sunday dinner was still an ongoing Johnson family tradition, even without Tim at the table. But over a short period of time, there was someone who, in a way, had replaced the empty space at the six-seater table in the dining room and had even given Deborah a helping hand in the kitchen.

Damien, David and Donovan happily prepared the dining room table and the plates, covering them with grilled lemon pepper chicken, asparagus, garlic mashed potatoes, and a buttered roll. The banana pudding sat on the island awaiting dessert time.

Donovan carried the pitchers of sweet tea and lemonade, David carried their mom's plate and Damien carried his girlfriend's plate.

"Thank you, baby," Deb said to David as he placed her plate in front of her.

"Thank you, baby," Kim said as Damien put the plate in front of her and kissed her lips.

"Get a room," Donovan said while rolling his eyes.

"Oh, hush Don. I am so excited to have Kim eating Sunday dinner with us. I hope this is the first of many more to come," Deborah said with unbelievable joy.

"Thank you for having me, Mrs. Johnson," Kim smiled.

"Just call me Ms. Deborah. I'll be dropping that last name as soon as my divorce is finalized."

There was an awkward silence from the other three Johnson men at the table.

"Yes, ma'am," said Kim.

"Can we eat?" asked David.

"Everyone bow your heads," Deb said. "Lord, we thank You for this beautiful meal You have blessed us with on Your day. Please allow it to nourish our bodies, our minds, and our souls. We pray for forgiveness and healing, oh Lord, for family, friends, and strangers the same. We thank You for life, love, and laughter, and pray that You provide them in abundance to us, Lord, for we will forever be grateful. These blessings we ask in Your name. Amen, amen, amen."

"Amen," everyone at the table said in unison.

They grabbed their silverware and began to dig into the freshly prepared food that sat atop their plates. No sooner than Damien could lift the fork to his mouth, his phone began to ring. His face scrunched up at the idea of who it could be. The people he loved and spoke to the most were sitting at the table with him and Sean was still in the hospital.

When he saw the name Cassie Campbell floating across his screen, he felt a wave of nervousness. Why would Sean's mom be calling? Could this be good news? Was he finally responsive or could it be a dreadful message?

"Hello?" Damien answered.

She could barely speak. She was overwhelmed with shock, tears and sorrow. "Dami-"

she sucked up snot in her nostrils and breathed heavily into the phone.

Harold took the phone from her. "Damien?"

"Yes, Mr. Campbell?"

"The doctors informed us that because of Sean's internal bleeding, there wasn't anything they could do. Sean is," there was hesitation in his voice, "no longer with us." Sean's dad began to cry and his mom's wailing could be heard through the receiver.

"Is that Cassie? What's wrong Damien?" Deborah asked.

"No!" Damien let out a painful howl. He dropped his phone and let his head fall down to the table. He didn't have to say a word. Everyone knew exactly what had just happened.

The mascara dripped down her face like wet paint on a wall. The rain poured and the tears that washed down her face disguised themselves as raindrops. She took the stairs, leaving a trail of water behind her with each step. When she reached the door, she stared at it for a moment before using the key he gave her to unlock and open it.

He stood in the kitchen in his Hanes boxer briefs making himself a turkey sandwich.

"Honey! You're soaking wet! Where's your umbrella? I thought it was my night to come over."

Joe was in complete shock to see Paula walking through the door, especially soaking wet. He knew it was raining, but she always kept an umbrella in her car, and she didn't call at all which was quite strange. "Paula, are you okay?"

He walked towards her and stood to her left peripheral, but she made no eye contact at the moment. She just stared straight ahead.

"Sean's dead," she said matter-of-factly.

Joe's eyes bulged in their sockets and his head dropped. "I'm really sorry to hear that." He embraced her, but her damp clothes made it difficult. "Let me get you a towel."

He returned with a blue beach-sized towel and draped it around her shoulders, creating a cape-like form around her. Still, she didn't budge.

"You're dead to me, too," she said coldly.

"What?" Joe asked, unsure if he heard her correctly.

"I know all about your little scheme with Tim. About how you tried to frame Deborah." She finally made eye contact with him. "About how you contacted Don't Shoot the Messenger and lied through your damn teeth to save some money." She paused for a moment and Joe remained silent. "And where did I fall into the equation? You probably knew the connection between them and me this whole time! You're nothing but a lying bastard!" Paula screamed at him.

"Paula…"

"Paula, what?! I don't wanna hear anything you have to say to me." She let the key fall from her hand to the cold tile floor. It chimed as it hit the floor and bounced twice before lying flat on the floor.

She turned and stormed out of the condo, allowing the hinges to cry out as she slammed the door behind her. Dejected, Joe didn't even have the strength in him to chase her. Everything he had inside left with Paula. Everything in him was gone. He may as well, as Paula said, have been dead just like Sean.

Chapter Twenty-One

Damien awoke with a heavy heart. No amount of time would have been enough to lay his best friend to his final resting place, but a week definitely didn't cut it. Sean and Damien had been best friends since they were eleven years old. They had done everything together, from riding bikes, to chasing girls down the street, to playing video games, to writing essays, to applying for college, to working in the same fast food joints, to trying weed and drinking underage, to learning how to drive and stealing their parents' cars in the middle of night, to starting a business together, and just the thought of not having Sean there anymore made Damien's eyes swell up with tears the size of ocean waves. The bereavement he'd go through he knew would last for years to come, maybe even for the rest of his natural life. He couldn't fathom, at least not at that moment, how he'd be able to cope with the loss.

He'd been to funerals before – great grands and aunts and uncles. Not that those people weren't important and didn't hold a special place in his heart, but it was just that he didn't have a connection to them like he did with Sean. He loved them; they were his family. But Sean was his best friend *and* his family, another brother. To lose him like this was more than devastating; it was torturous.

Sean's parents, Cassie and Harold, asked everyone to wear a combination of black and white – white to celebrate Sean's life and black to grieve the loss of their only child.

Damien stood in the driveway in black Stacy Adams', black slacks, a white Ralph Lauren long sleeve button up, and a black diamond stitched tie. He stood in a crowd of people, mostly Sean's family, feeling lost, alone and withdrawn from the world. But when it was time to pray, he grabbed the nearest two hands, bowed his head, and closed his eyes so tight that they began to water.

Afterwards, the drivers held the doors to the limousines open for the family and close friends to fill inside and proceed to the church. The long, stretched cars were filled with melancholy faces, runny noses, watery eyes, and silence. The ten minute ride seemed like a cross-country road trip.

When they arrived to the church, there was already a packed house with friends, associates, and coworkers from near and far. The first five pews on the left were reserved for family and close family friends.

Damien took his seat at the end of the row on the navy blue cushion. He sat straight up, tense and uneasy. He glanced down at the obituary that he held tightly in his moist hand.

The obituary had been done very well. A recent photo of Sean centered the front page along with the dates of his sunrise and sunset, a scripture from Psalm 116:15, and the church that would be holding the funeral processions. The inside included a short biography, friends and family left behind, and the program agenda. The back page concluded with the pallbearers, one of whom was Damien, and a poem dedicated to Sean.

The space around the casket was adorned with flowers and pictures. A photograph of Sean and Paula caught Damien's eye. He scanned the room until he spotted Paula sitting in between her parents and Angie and Michelle. They caught eyes and made a waving gesture to one another.

There were several pictures with Sean and him, but the one that really stood out was the one from the day they graduated from college. They wore the largest smiles that day, graduating and celebrating together. It was a huge deal because there were a few times he thought he wouldn't graduate at all. The university had put him on academic probation on more than one occasion. He was so busy clubbing and chasing girls that he'd lost focus of what was really important. He'd pull all-nighters in hopes of finishing an assignment only to complete it so poorly that he'd earn a D or F on it. Sean had always been the more studious of the two of them, but college had really set them apart. Their junior year, Sean sat Damien down and truly expressed his concern for his best friend. He helped Damien turn his below average academic situation into a positive one. Well, one good enough to walk across the stage and shake hands with the president of the university and receive his degree. And on graduation day, Sean was right there rooting him on.

Graduating college was one of the most fulfilling events in Damien's life. The other was starting a business. But as a result of that venture, he sat there in the pew staring at Sean's body in the open black casket. Damien was sure he was going to drain his body of every drop of liquid if he didn't get ahold of his emotions. He spent most of his life trying not to show too much emotion and now it seemed as if he had no control at all.

The choir stole everyone's attention as they began filing in the stands. The pastor entered the church from a side entrance door. He welcomed everyone and began the services with a meaningful prayer. The choir then took over with their first song, a classic that the whole church would be able to join in and sing along to.

"Why should I feel discouraged? And why should the shadows come?" The lyrics to His Eye is on the Sparrow rang through the church, filling the quiet spaces and empty hearts with peace and optimism. There was hardly a dry eye in the entire building by the end of the song. But when the choir began to sing, "I Feel Like Going On", people began rising to their feet. Not only were they having a home going service for Sean, but they were starting to have church.

Although he allowed the words to travel through his soul, Damien still questioned whether or not he felt like going on, particularly in reference to the business. Don't Shoot the Messenger had proven to be a small success and was on a continuous growth spurt. But with one of the messengers actually having been shot, Damien knew deep down that he was completely done.

Damien had been so deep in thought that he hadn't even realized it was time for him to go to the pulpit and give his eulogy. All eyes, from every color on the eye-color spectrum, were on him. Hands came together as people began to encourage him to get up and give his speech.

He slowly rose to his feet and exited the pew to the right, walking down the middle of the church. After about ten steps forward and three steps up, he was in the pulpit. He took his place behind the clear, glass podium and looked out into the crowd. He reluctantly pulled the paper out of his right pocket, unfolded it and placed it on the podium. He flattened the paper out with both hands and tried to clear the knot out of his throat before he began to speak.

"Good morning," Damien mumbled. He cleared his throat and tried again. "Good morning." He spoke clearly into the mic that time, so the church responded.

"Good morning," everyone said altogether.

"I'll be honest with you all. I did not want to do this. I did not want to get up here behind this podium and say one word, and if it wasn't for Mrs. Campbell's pleas, I wouldn't be up here. I didn't want to have to say my last words and basically say goodbye to my friend." He paused, and his head dropped.

"If you know anything about me and Sean, you know that we've been best friends since we were eleven. One thing I can say about Sean is that he's always been loyal. People could always depend on him and he always kept his word. As kids, we lived by the code: Bros before …" he paused and the crowd laughed lightly, "…girls. But then he met this girl named Paula and she changed the game up. I can't even lie. At first, I hated on their relationship, especially as I saw it blossoming and becoming more serious. And I hate to admit it now, but it wasn't until after they broke up that I realized what they had was real love and how much I wanted, and want, that for myself."

He paused again, looking out into the crowd. He spotted Paula, wiping the constant flow of tears from her face. Then he spotted Kim. She'd come to support him, sitting in the very last pew of the church. She met his eyes with hers and gave him a smile.

"My parents blessed me with twin brothers, and I love my brothers. But twins, especially identical twins, have this special bond, and even though I never outwardly expressed it, I always felt like a third wheel with them. The Campbell's blessed me with more than just a friend; they blessed me with another brother. I'm going to miss his friendship, our brotherhood, the loyalty, the –" Damien's eyes were welling up again and the words on his paper were becoming blurry. He stood silent for what felt like one full moon phase around the earth. The crowd, again, began to clap him on. He could hear a distant, "It's alright!" from a female somewhere in the back of the church. An, "Amen!" was shouted out as well. Damien took a deep breath and prepared to speak again.

"Sean Maurice Campbell, my brother from another mother, may you rest in peace. Your memory will forever live in me."

The crowd clapped heavily as Damien ended his heartfelt eulogy to Sean. He felt several pats on his back as he returned to his end seat on the fourth pew.

The memorial service continued with more music, words of encouragement and remembrance, and a final word from the pastor. Many people had sent their condolences to Sean's family. One of the female ushers read all of the notes that came with the tons of floral arrangements that sat around the casket as if protecting it from harm.

The lid of the casket was shut and it was time for the pallbearers, as they carried Sean, to lead the way out of the church. The six men, Damien and five of Sean's cousins, gently placed the casket in the back of the hearse, which would lead the procession to the burial site. Everyone filed in their cars, following the leader and driving very slowly. It looked like a long line of ants returning to the mound after a long journey to report back to the queen. Sean was on his way to report back to the King after what seemed like a journey cut short.

Cars stopped in the road as the procession passed by, making its way to the cemetery. Damien could see a little boy's face pressed against the driver's side back seat window. Damien read confusion on the boy's face as he looked in amazement at the dozens of cars passing by in a single file line, but noticing all the other cars stopped.

The lips of the woman in the driver's seat moved, and the little boy pulled his face from the window and sat back down.

The gravesite awaited as the fleet of vehicles approached. There was a tent, under which were eight chairs and the six foot deep hole that would house the casket that held Sean's cold body.

The casket was gently placed on the casket lowering device. Dozens of guests gathered around the tent while Cassie, Harold, Sean's paternal grandmother and grandfather, his maternal grandmother, and a couple of aunts and uncles filled the eight seats underneath.

Damien stood near the tent, positioning himself just so to block the sunlight from shining in his eyes. The weather was too beautiful to be such a gloomy day. He stared at the pastor who held the Bible and three red roses in his hands.

The spoken words of the pastor floated in the air, leaving an inevitable trail as they passed by Damien's ears. All of Damien's senses were paused except his sense of sight. The sound of crying was drowned out by the smell of tears hitting the air. The taste of sorrow was buried by the touch of grief. Damien could only see the pastor's lips moving, see the Campbell's wiping their tears away, and the heartache that everyone wore on their shoulders. And then came the sight that would live with him forever, the lowering of the casket. Its descend was slow, yet deliberate. It was, indeed, the last chapter and final scene of Sean's life.

As the memorial services were finally coming to an end, Damien turned and looked in search of a small green Toyota Corolla. Once he spotted it, he made a mad dash to the passenger side of the car.

Kim leaned over to unlock the manual door for Damien to get in.

She held both arms out to embrace him tightly and asked, "You okay?"

"I will be," Damien replied.

Kim put the car in gear, but just before she could drive off, Damien blurted out, "I love you."

She looked at him, making direct eye contact. The conversation they had with their eyes lasted for an everlasting minute, and he reassured her through his that he was serious.

Smiling, she returned the sweet words of affection, "I love you, too."

Epilogue

1 Year Later

When Don't Shoot the Messenger finally came to an end directly following Sean's funeral, Damien found himself training fulltime again. He didn't mind at first because the weight lifting and cardio seemed to fill his empty void, and when that didn't do it, Kim was always there. Damien's first experience at being in love had been a fulfilling one, even in his time of weakness. She filled him with strength.

He found himself at times randomly wanting to perform nice gestures for Kim just because. It didn't have to be an anniversary or special occasion, it just had to be a day the good Lord had made.

One evening out at Phillips Pork Palace for a special, no reason at all, dinner for two, Damien spotted Paula.

"Baby, remember Sean's ex, Paula, from the funeral?" She nodded her head up and down. "There she is." He pointed and looked in her direction.

She was walking through the restaurant back to her table after having used the restroom. She smiled as she approached the dimly lit table where Joe awaited. He returned the smile and stood up to pull out her chair.

"Oh, shit. They're still together," Damien said, wide-eyed.

"Love conquers all," Kim said with a smile.

The waiter approached to take their drink orders, and they both ordered a lemon water to start.

Damien grabbed her left hand, lifted it to his lips, and gave it a tender kiss. "Speaking of love, I had an idea that I wanted to share with you."

"I'm listening," Kim smiled.

He paused momentarily, but went on. "It's another business, except this time with a focus on love and bringing people together rather than breaking people up. It was you, actually, who gave me the idea. And because 'love conquers all', I think it would eventually be a lot more successful than Don't Shoot the Messenger. There's only one thing…"

"What's that?" Kim asked.

"I want you to be my business partner. I can't have a business about love without having you involved." He looked at her with glaring and pleading eyes seeking approval.

"Of course I'll be your business partner, babe," Kim replied, smiling from ear to ear.

Damien was relieved. He had no reason to believe that she'd turn him down, but he was glad she wanted to help him make this new business venture a success.

"Now, we need a name and game plan. Name first," Damien said.

"Babe, now you know I have to eat first to get these creative juices flowing."

"How about The Love Conquerors?" Damien suggested.

A smidgen of Kim's water squirted out of her mouth as she tried to control her laughter. "That's so cheesy." She waved her right hand in the air to get the waiter's attention. "We're gonna need food *and* drinks from the bar for this," Kim teased.

The waiter took their orders, and the couple spent the rest of the evening eating, drinking, laughing, and coming up with a name for the next best business venture that would this time be filled with life, love, and laughter.

About the Author

Ashara graduated from Florida State University with a Bachelor's of Science in English Education. She has been a middle school language arts teacher for six years. She currently teaches and lives in Atlanta, GA with her daughter, Trinity. *Don't Shoot the Messenger* is Ashara's debut novel.

Follow her on:

Facebook *@Don't Shoot the Messenger* or

Instagram *@AsharaD16*

84167797R00118

Made in the USA
Middletown, DE
17 August 2018